# *Not Until*

# *Forever*

## A Hope Springs Novel

# Valerie M. Bodden

## Hope Springs Series

Not Until Forever

Not Until This Moment

Not Until You

Not Until Us

Not Until Christmas Morning

Not Until This Day

Not Until Someday

Not Until Now

Not Until Then

Not Until The End

## River Falls Series

Pieces of Forever

Songs of Home

Memories of the Heart

Whispers of Truth

Promises of Mercy

## River Falls Christmas Romances

Christmas of Joy

# A Hope Springs Gift for You

Members of my Reader's Club get a FREE book, available exclusively to my subscribers. When you sign up, you'll also be the first to know about new releases, book deals, and giveaways.

Visit www.valeriembodden.com/gift to join!

But when the kindness and love of God our Savior appeared, he saved us, not because of righteous things we had done, but because of his mercy.

Titus 3:4-5

# Prologue

Spencer paced behind the park bench, tipping his head toward the gray clouds swirling above him. His nerves swirled faster. He patted at the pocket of his hoodie for the eighth time, letting the solidity of the little box there reassure him. Even if some parts of his life were falling apart right now, this was the one thing he was sure of.

He squinted toward the parking lot, watching for the flash of Sophie's bright red Camaro. But the lot was empty, aside from his battered pickup truck, already packed with the few things he needed from his apartment. It was hard to believe he was going to walk away without his degree with less than a semester to go. But this was what he had to do. His family needed him.

He scrubbed a hand over his face and made himself sit down. He should be on his way already. But he couldn't leave without doing this. Without telling Sophie what he wanted for the future. Their future.

Finally, the rumble of the Camaro's engine caught his ears. Spencer fumbled at his pocket again as Sophie whipped into the parking lot. The wind unfurled her golden hair behind her as she stepped out of the car. Spencer shoved a hand roughly through his own hair and swallowed hard. What had he been thinking, doing this here?

He should have picked somewhere more romantic. More elegant. More Sophie. But this park had been their place since their first date three years ago. It was where they came to talk, to laugh, to share everything. Doing this here, now, felt right. Spencer forced himself to take a slow breath as Sophie hurried toward him, her strides long and sure in her heels and slim black skirt.

Just the sight of her lightened his heart. He had no idea what a woman like her saw in a man like him, but he'd learned not to question it. For whatever reason, they worked. And for that, he thanked God.

Spencer sank his face into her hair as his arms tugged her closer. This was what he'd needed. Whatever he was facing, holding Sophie made everything right in the world.

She pulled back a few inches and slid her fingers over his unshaven cheek. "You look tired. You sure you want to make the drive back to Hope Springs yet tonight?"

Not now that he was with her, he didn't. But he nodded. "I have to, Soph."

He'd only been home a couple of days—just long enough to sit with Mom through the worst of the waiting at the hospital. Through the hours of not knowing if Dad would make it.

Sophie looked away, but not before he caught the flash of disappointment in her eyes. "How's your dad?"

Spencer disentangled from her embrace and grabbed her hand, leading her around the muddy patches toward their favorite spot at the edge of the park's little pond. A family of ducks quacked at them and shuffled out of the way.

"He's stable. Should be out of the hospital in a few days, but he's not going to be back in the orchard anytime soon." He couldn't push away the image of Dad's gray face. His slow movements. How could a heart attack have transformed his powerhouse of a dad so drastically?

Sophie bit her lip in that way that made it almost impossible to resist kissing her. "It's just so close to graduation. It seems like a waste to throw away everything you've worked for."

Spencer sighed. He'd had this argument with himself all the way here. But he couldn't see any way around it.

"The work won't wait, Soph. The seasons keep changing, no matter what's going on in our lives." He squeezed her hand. "Anyway, it's not like if I don't finish my degree now I can't ever do it. I have my whole life." *Our whole life*. But he was getting ahead of himself.

"I know." Sophie offered a half-hearted smile. "I just hate the idea of saying goodbye sooner than we planned."

He pulled her to a stop next to the bench they'd spent so many hours on. "Me too. That's actually why I asked you to come here."

He gestured for her to sit, and she did, giving him a curious look as he remained on his feet. He drew in a shaky breath. He'd been so busy thinking about everything else that he hadn't prepared what to say.

"There's something I have to ask you."

A wind gust blew her hair in front of her face, and she swept it behind her ear as he dropped to one knee. Hands shaking, he pulled the ring box from his pocket, opened it, and held the small diamond solitaire toward her.

Sophie gasped, lifting a hand to her mouth. "Spencer, don't—"

"Sophie, will you—" Spencer stopped as her words slammed into him. "What?"

Sophie sprang to her feet and practically leaped over the bench, as if trying to construct a physical barrier between them. "You're emotional right now. You're not thinking clearly."

Spencer pushed slowly to his feet and moved closer to the bench, reaching for Sophie's hand across its back. "I'm not doing this because I'm emotional. I already had the ring. I was planning to wait until graduation, but with everything going on, I wanted you to know that I want a future with you."

He squeezed her hand and tried to pull her around the bench so he could try again and this time do it properly. Leave it to him to screw up the proposal the first time.

But Sophie pulled out of his grasp and looked past him, toward the pond.

Spencer's heart crumbled. She didn't want to marry him.

"I'm leaving for Chicago in two months, Spencer. You know I can't pass up this job offer."

He wanted to tell her it didn't matter. That he'd go with her. Or he'd find her a job that was just as good closer to home. Anything.

But admitting his need would only lead to more hurt. Would only remind him that he'd never be worthy of her.

"I'm sorry," Sophie whispered.

And then she turned and walked away.

And he let her.

# Chapter 1

*Five Years Later*

Sophie stepped off the L, deftly dodging the enormous puddles on the sidewalk from last night's rain so she wouldn't ruin her new Jimmy Choo heels. She inhaled deeply, trying to catch a hint of spring. But spring in Chicago smelled nothing like spring at home in Hope Springs. There, the season carried the heady scents of ice melt and earth and fruit blossoms. Here, all she could smell were exhaust fumes and the overripe garbage bins that had been set out on the sidewalk for pickup.

It didn't matter—she'd likely be inside all day and long into the night anyway. This new development was the biggest deal she'd worked on yet, and with any luck, it was the one that would secure her promotion as the firm's youngest VP. It didn't matter how much time she had to spend indoors or how many hours it took. She'd make it happen.

She pushed through the doors of the sleek glass tower on North Clark and hurried across the lobby, relishing the sharp click of her heels against the polished marble floor. She still couldn't believe sometimes that she'd landed a position with Heartland, one of the most prestigious development firms in the country.

"Good morning, Sophie," the white-haired security guard greeted her as he did every morning.

"Morning," Sophie mumbled as she hurried past and jabbed at the elevator's up button.

At the twenty-eighth floor, she stepped out into the posh lobby of Heartland and made her way to her office. As always, her eyes were drawn immediately to the breathtaking view of the city and the Lake Michigan shoreline. There was a slight chop on the water today, though the waves winked in the sun.

Not that she had time to stand here and admire the view. Sophie settled into her leather chair and grabbed the project she'd been working on for two weeks. She leafed through the papers. This was her first project as lead developer, and she had a lot riding on it. But if she could pull off the purchase and development of the combination apartment, shopping, and entertainment complex she'd envisioned . . .

*One step at a time, Sophie. When you get ahead of yourself, you get sloppy.* How many times had her mom used that reprimand on her growing up? It seemed to apply to everything from math tests to ballet recitals. Somehow, nothing she did had ever been good enough for her parents.

She shook herself. She'd never earn her promotion if she focused on the past instead of the task at hand. She pulled out the latest renderings from the architect and dove in.

An hour later, a rap on her door made her jump.

"Staff meeting, three minutes." Her assistant Tina passed her a fresh cup of coffee.

"Ah, thanks." Sophie smoothed her hair and shuffled the papers she'd spread across her desk into a neat pile. Then she gathered the whole bunch and hurried to the conference room.

The firm's six other developers were already gathered around the room's large mahogany table. This room was definitely the most intimidating in the office, with its oversize table and chairs that seemed to swallow her, but Sophie kept her chin up as she entered the room and grabbed a seat next to Chase. He gave her a warm smile and a subtle wink.

She ducked her head to hide her blush. Not that it was a big secret that the two had been casually dating. But Sophie felt awkward when he acted like that at work—especially in front of his father, who also happened to be one of the partners.

"Glad you could make it, Sophie." Mr. Davis's joke barely masked a hard edge of irritation.

"Sorry, I got caught up in the Hudson project."

Mr. Sanders, who'd always been the friendlier of the two partners, turned to her. "How does it look? Everything on track?"

Sophie patted the folder in front of her. "I think so. But—"

"Excuse me." All eyes swiveled to Tina as she poked her head into the room.

Sophie gestured for her to step back outside. Heartland had a strict policy about interruptions during meetings. As in, you didn't do it. Ever.

"I'm sorry." Tina motioned to Sophie. "You have a phone call. It's your grandmother."

"My grandmother?" She hadn't talked to Nana in months—and never at work. A slice of fear cut through her. It must be an emergency. Her mouth went dry, but she pushed her chair back and mumbled an apology, not sure if her words were audible.

Once she was out of the conference room, she sped across the common area to her office.

She lunged for her phone and snatched it off the desk, hitting the flashing button. "Nana?" The word came out breathless, as if she'd just finished a marathon cardio Pilates session.

"There's my Sophie." Her grandmother's voice rasped through the phone.

"Nana, is everything okay? Of course it's not okay or you wouldn't be calling me at work in the middle of the day. Is it Mom? Or Dad?" What if it was both of them—a car accident, maybe, on one of the rare occasions they were actually together.

"I knew you'd make time for me." Nana's words sounded garbled, and Sophie felt as if she'd been dropped into the middle of a foreign movie.

"Make time for you? Nana, what's the emergency?"

"I just wanted to hear your voice."

Sophie held the phone away from her ear and gave it an incredulous stare. Nana had interrupted her meeting to hear her voice? She rubbed at her temple as she pulled the phone back to her ear. "It's so good to hear from you, Nana, but I'm actually in the middle of a meeting." She glanced at the clock above her door. "I'll call you back in an hour or so, okay?"

She was met with silence.

"Nana?"

"Do me a favor, Sophie."

Sophie drummed her fingers on her desk. Now wasn't the best time for favors. "You got it, Nana. Whatever it is, I'm on it. Just as soon as my meeting is over. I'll—"

"Remember that I love you and so does God." Nana's voice was getting fainter, as if she was holding the phone too far from her mouth. Sophie strained to hear. "If you remember that, then I've done my job. Okay, Sophie?"

"Okay, Nana." Sophie didn't really have time for Nana's philosophical musings right now. "I have to go. I'll call you—"

"That's okay, Sophie. You don't have to call back. I just wanted to hear your voice one more time before I go."

"Go?" A brainstorm about the Hudson project hit Sophie, and she reached for a pen and a sticky note to jot it down. "Are you taking a trip?"

Nana was always going somewhere or other.

"I'm going home, Sophie."

"Hmm." Sophie finished her note. "Where are you now?" Probably the Mediterranean or somewhere in East Asia. She'd probably forgotten the time difference.

"I'm in the hospital, dear."

Sophie dropped her pen and straightened. Nana had been battling cancer for a couple years and had ended up in the hospital more than once in that time. Still, Sophie knew how much she hated being cooped up.

"But you get to go home soon? That's good news."

"Not that home, dear." Nana's voice was overly gentle, like it had been the first time Sophie came to her with a broken heart.

"What do you mean, 'not that home'? What other home do you have?" Sophie frowned. She hadn't noticed any decline in Nana's mental ability, but much as she hated to face it, Nana *was* getting older.

"I mean, I don't think I'll see that home again. I'm going to my true home."

"True home?" This conversation was making less sense by the minute.

Nana sighed, and Sophie felt like she'd missed something important, but she couldn't for the life of her think what it could be.

"Heaven, dear. I'm going home to heaven."

Sophie's head jerked up as she sat hard in her desk chair. She opened and closed her mouth a few times before she could get any words out. "You don't know that, Nana. I'm sure you have lots of time left. You—"

"You can't argue my way out of this, Sophie." Nana's chuckle grated against Sophie's nerves. How could she deliver news like this and then laugh?

"How long—?" Sophie swallowed the boulder that had lodged in her throat.

"A couple of days, the doctors think. Maybe a week."

"I'm sorry, Nana." Her voice was barely a whisper. She fought off the sharp sting gathering behind her eyes. If she didn't cry, she wouldn't feel. It was a skill she'd perfected over the years.

"Don't you be sorry for me, child." Nana's voice was firm. "I know where I'm going. And I got to say goodbye to my Sophie. That's all I asked. God is good."

Sophie chewed her lip. A phone call was no way to say goodbye to the woman who'd been almost a mother to her. Who had loved her unconditionally her whole life, even when her own parents hadn't.

"I'll be on my way in ten minutes. Do you think you could—" Sophie sucked in a breath. "Could you wait for me? Before you—" But she refused to finish that sentence.

"It's in God's hands, dear."

It wasn't the guarantee Sophie had been hoping for, but it would have to do. She hung up and took a minute to steel herself. Then she pushed slowly to her feet and walked to Mr. Sanders's office, taking a steadying breath before she knocked on his door.

Chase was already in with his father, but Mr. Sanders invited her in as well.

She waited for one of them to say something about the phone call, but when neither did, she pushed forward. "I need to request a few days off. That was my grandmother who called—" Sophie cut herself off. No need to remind them of the interruption to the meeting. "Anyway, she's not doing well. The doctors only give her a few days." She didn't let herself dwell on the words. "I'd like to go home. To say goodbye."

Chase toed the floor, not meeting her eyes.

"Are you close to your grandmother?" Mr. Sanders's voice was neither compassionate nor judgmental. It was a solid neutral.

"I am. Or, well, I was. I haven't been to visit her in a while . . ." Sophie cleared her throat.

"You understand how important this project is? To the firm as well as to your career?" Mr. Sanders folded his hands in front of him on the desk.

Sophie bit her lip, nodding.

"Then—" Mr. Sanders stood, and Sophie understood the move as a dismissal. "I'll leave it up to you. If you stay, you keep the project. If you go, I'm going to put Chase on it. We can't afford to lose out on this one, and if you can't dedicate yourself to it one hundred percent . . ."

Sophie blinked at the unfairness. He was going to make her choose between her family and her career?

She ducked out of her office, her insides roiling. How was she supposed to make a decision like this?

Halfway across the lobby, Chase caught up with her. "Sophie, wait. What are you going to do?" She couldn't tell if that was eagerness in his voice or compassion.

"I guess I'm going to—" The word stay almost came out. It's what she should do. For her own good. But the image of Nana, alone in her hospital bed, pushed into her head. Could she really forgive herself if she let Nana die alone like that? "I'm going to go. I'll get you the plans."

To his credit, Chase didn't gloat or even smile. "For what it's worth, Sophie, I'm sorry. I know how much you wanted this project."

She shrugged. "There'll be others." Of course, she could kiss that VP position goodbye. If Chase hadn't been a shoo-in before, he certainly would be after this.

She stepped around him and into her office, grabbing the stack of plans for the Hudson project off her desk. She passed it to Chase. "I should get going."

He gave her hand a quick squeeze. "Don't be gone too long. Maybe you can help me put the finishing touches on the project plan."

Sophie nodded and stepped out of the office toward the bank of elevators.

She had no intention of staying in Hope Springs a moment longer than she had to.

⌒⌒

The lowering sun lit the water on fire as Sophie crested the hill above Hope Springs five hours later.

She pulled down the Camaro's sun visor and rubbed at her weary eyes.

As the road dropped into the town, she slowed, letting herself take in sights she hadn't seen in more than five years.

It was odd how everything looked the same and yet different. It wasn't yet tourist season, so most of the shops were closed for the evening, and the streets were mostly empty, aside from the occasional local walking their dog.

Memories piled up and slammed into her as she passed the Hidden Cafe. The Chocolate Chicken. The post office. Sophie tried to beat them back. She wasn't here to reminisce. She was here to say goodbye to Nana and then get back to her real life.

She accelerated, trying to leave the memories behind as she passed out of town. Her stomach tightened into double knots as she pulled into the long, winding driveway that led up the highest bluff overlooking the lake. Bare trees pressed in on her from all sides, until her parents' over-large house finally came into view, all hard lines and sharp angles.

She parked in the large section of the driveway her parents reserved for guests and sat for a minute, gazing toward the now-dark waters of the lake. Was this really the same lake she'd been looking at hours ago from her office in Chicago? It was the one thing that connected her two lives. That and the memories. But those she tried not to think about.

She forced herself to push her car door open. To grab her suitcase out of the trunk. To follow the slate path to the front door.

She reached for the doorknob but then thought better of it and pressed her finger to the doorbell.

When no one answered after a minute, she let herself in. "Hello?" She felt oddly like an intruder as her voice echoed around her childhood home.

"In here." Mom's voice carried from the kitchen.

Sophie left her suitcase in the foyer and followed the sound.

Mom was seated at the long granite breakfast counter, poring over a design magazine. She barely glanced up when Sophie entered. "I told you, you didn't have to come."

"I wanted to come." Sophie gave her mother an obligatory kiss on the cheek.

She knew better than to ask where her father was. If her mother was home, her father was likely at the club. The two had barely been in the same room together, aside from at church and when brokering real estate deals, in the past fifteen years.

"How's Nana?" Sophie went to the refrigerator and grabbed a bottle of water.

"Call her grandmother." Sophie's mom gave an exaggerated huff. "You know I hate when you call her Nana. Sounds like that dog from that movie."

"Peter Pan?" Sophie wrinkled her nose. She'd been calling her grandmother Nana since she was seven. She wasn't about to stop now. "Have you been to see her?"

"I called earlier. There's no change." Mom flipped the page of her magazine. "I don't know what you think being here is going to accomplish. You should have stayed at work."

Sophie took another sip of her water to keep from striking back. It was the same old story. Her parents would never be satisfied with anything she did.

"I wanted to say goodbye." She focused on keeping an even tone.

Her mother nodded, eyes fixed on her magazine. "I'm thinking about redoing the kitchen. What do you think of these cabinets?"

Sophie set her water on the counter and walked out of the room without looking at the magazine. "They're nice, Mom."

She grabbed her suitcase and trudged up the staircase before her mother could infuriate her any more. Not that Mom had ever been emotionally available, but planning to redecorate the kitchen while her own mother was dying was too much even for her.

At the end of the hallway, Sophie pushed open the door to her old room. It'd been completely redone as a guest room almost the moment she left for college. All her old posters had been stripped from the walls. The poppy orange she'd painted the room when she was fifteen had been replaced by a soft lilac. She had to admit that the room was more to her taste now, but seeing it stripped of her former self stung.

Oh, well. It's not like she could ever go back to who she used to be.

Sophie hefted her suitcase onto the overstuffed chair in the corner and collapsed on the king-size bed. That was new, too. She longed for the twin-size canopy bed she'd gotten from her grandmother—it'd been the one place that always felt cozy in the cold house.

After a few minutes, she grew restless. She'd had way too much coffee on the way up. She wouldn't be able to sleep for hours yet, but the thought of returning to the kitchen and doing another round with Mom turned her stomach. She crossed to the room's built-in bookshelf. When she'd lived here, it'd overflowed with books. Mysteries, mostly. Romance. Some classics.

Now, it held mostly knickknacks, but a few books were sprinkled here and there. She ran her fingers over the spines until they landed on *Pride and Prejudice*. Had this really been her favorite book once? Had she really believed that two people who were so different, who came from such different backgrounds, could make a life together? Well, Jane Austen may have been that naive, but she wasn't. Not anymore.

Still, she couldn't resist pulling the worn copy off the shelf. A bookmark stuck out about a third of the way through the book.

As she flipped to the page, something small and white fluttered out and drifted to the floor.

She bent to pick it up, and her breath caught.

It was a pressed cherry blossom, in pristine condition.

From Spencer. When he gave it to her, he said it reminded him of her—strong and delicate at the same time.

She gently lifted the blossom to her face. A faint scent of spring lingered on it. Or maybe that was just wishful thinking.

She replaced the blossom in the book and stuck it on the shelf. That part of her life was over.

Besides, Spencer likely had a wife and family of his own by now.

A pang sliced through her belly. What if she ran into him while she was home? Worse, what if she ran into his new family? Could she handle seeing him with another woman?

She shook her head and flopped onto the bed. She was being ridiculous. It wouldn't matter if she saw him and his family or not.

She had a highly successful career, an upscale apartment, a casual boyfriend who didn't expect anything long-term from her. She had everything she had ever wanted.

Which didn't explain the hollow feeling that had taken up residence in her chest.

# Chapter 2

Spencer grabbed a cherry branch and pulled it closer to his face. The wood that had appeared barren from a distance showed little signs of new life all along its length, tiny buds just barely poking out from the bark.

Spencer ran his fingers over them. They were no guarantee that the tree would actually blossom and fruit, but it was a good sign.

A sign they needed right now.

He stepped back to survey the tree, choosing the branches he'd prune. He needed to choose carefully. Last year, a late season frost had destroyed their entire crop. If they hadn't had his woodworking to fall back on, the farm probably would have gone under entirely.

But cherries were the lifeblood of the peninsula, drawing tourists from all over the state. If the crop failed this year—

He couldn't think about that.

He grabbed his pruning saw and lifted it to a dead branch. With a practiced rhythm, his saw bit into the wood until the branch came off clean in his fist. He slathered sealant on the fresh wood underneath to prevent disease, then selected another branch to prune. Spencer let himself fall into the familiar routine of spring on the orchard as he shaped the tree, ensuring maximum air flow and sunlight to the branches. When he'd finished, he gathered his fallen branches and dragged them toward the trailer he and Dad had been filling all morning.

Dad was taking the lopping shears to a tree near the pile. Spencer still had to think about each cut he made, consider the tree before choosing a branch to trim, but for his father, it was second nature. He never hesitated, just snipped branch after branch until the trees were shaped perfectly.

"Slow down, Dad. You're making me look bad."

Dad grunted and lowered his shears, rubbing at the left side of his chest. He shifted to lean his weight heavily against the tree trunk.

"Dad?" Spencer moved closer. "You okay?"

Sweat gleamed on Dad's face, despite the chill breeze that blew in off the lake. He waved Spencer off. "Fine. Just need a break for a second." He pushed off the trunk and set back to work.

Spencer studied him. Since he could remember, Dad had always been the first to work and the last to quit. But he'd slowed down some in the years since his heart attack. "Why don't you go back to the house for a bit? I've got this. Give me a chance to catch up."

His father kept clipping. "Stop coddling me. I get enough of that from your mother." He lowered the shears again to roll out his left shoulder, then lifted it to the next branch.

"I'm not coddling, Dad. But you know Mom would never forgive me if—"

"You let me worry about your mother. I don't need a break, and I'm not going to take one. In case you've forgotten, we've got a whole orchard to get ready. We don't have time to stand here arguing."

He wasn't wrong about that. Last year's lost crop meant they didn't have the money to hire on any seasonal help this year. Dad bent and gathered his discarded branches. Spencer reached to help him.

"I said I can do it." His father's voice held the sharp edge of warning Spencer recognized from his childhood.

"All right, Dad." Spencer raised his hands and moved to the other side of the row to trim the next tree. Arguing would only make it worse.

Spencer's phone rang, overly loud in the silent orchard, and he pulled it out of his pocket, answering as he examined the tree.

"What's up, Dave?"

Their neighbor from the next farm over huffed into the phone, and Spencer waited for him to catch his breath. Dave was older than Dad, but he still insisted on doing all his work himself. Spencer always worried that one of these days it would kill him.

"Having an issue with Old Bessie over here," Dave puffed. "She's bottomed out pretty good. Think you could come over and help me push her out?"

Spencer's shoulders tightened. Helping Dave with the tractor would put him back at least an hour. And this orchard wasn't going to prune itself. But if the situation were reversed, Dave would be over in a second. And if his father had taught him anything, it was that neighbors were a farmer's lifeline. "Yeah, Dave. I'll be right over."

He jabbed his phone into his pocket and stalked toward the ATV he and Dad had ridden out to the orchard. He unhitched the trailer from it and lowered it to the ground.

"Gotta go help Dave with Old Bessie," he called to his father.

Dad waved to acknowledge he'd heard but kept working his saw. Spencer almost asked one more time if he was okay but bit the question back. Having his head torn off twice in one day wasn't worth it. He jumped on the ATV and took off toward the field that bordered Dave's farm. Mud from the rains that had saturated the ground the last few weeks shot up at him, but he pushed the machine harder. He had too much to do today to worry about getting a little dirty.

Ten minutes later, he found Dave knee-deep in mud, slogging around his old, beat-up tractor.

The ground sucked at Spencer's feet as he jumped off the ATV.

"Gonna need to invest in a new tractor one of these days," he called to Dave.

Dave grunted. "Not ready to give up on Old Bessie yet."

Spencer pulled out the chains he kept in the ATV's storage compartment. He passed one end to Dave. When everything was secure, he jumped on the machine and gunned it. He gritted his teeth and squinted against the mud spraying up around him, throttling up higher.

But after half an hour, the old beast remained stuck.

Spencer switched off the ATV. No sense killing it, too. He pulled out his phone. "Gonna have to call in the old man for reinforcements," he called to Dave.

He scrolled to Dad's number. But the phone rang until it went to voice mail.

Spencer frowned and dialed again. He clenched his teeth as the rings added up. Voice mail again.

Something heavy dropped in Spencer's stomach. He shouldn't have left Dad alone. He'd promised Mom. It didn't matter that Dad had been in perfect health for the past five years. Didn't matter that his mood had made it easier for Spencer to walk away. If something had happened to him—

Spencer reined in his thoughts.

Just because Dad wasn't answering his phone didn't mean anything bad had happened. He probably didn't have his phone on him. He was forever leaving it at home or in the shed.

But Spencer couldn't stop picturing how Dad had been rubbing at his chest, rolling his shoulder, sweating. Weren't those exactly the signs he was supposed to watch for?

With a sudden decisiveness, Spencer jumped off the ATV and worked to free it from the chains.

"What's up?" Dave called.

"Dad's not answering. I'm going to go check on him. I'll be—"

But Dave was at his side, a hand on his shoulder. "Let me do this."

Spencer didn't stop to think. Just dropped the chains his shaking hands had been unable to unhitch and jumped on the ATV, bringing it roaring to life. The moment Dave said "go," he shot off.

The machine whined as he pushed it to its limits, barely noticing the branches that whipped at his face as he raced the ATV through the thin stand of trees between their farm and Dave's.

*Please let me get there in time.* He repeated the prayer over and over as he maneuvered the ATV closer. Why couldn't the machine go any faster?

Finally, he reached the orchard. He jumped off the ATV, swiveling his head toward the spot Dad was working last. But the orchard was empty.

*He probably went back to the house for a break, like you told him to.*

But Spencer knew in his gut Dad wouldn't have taken that advice.

"Dad?" He ran down the long line of trees, trying not to let the panic that clawed at him take over. How far could Dad have gotten?

"Dad?" When he'd gone a hundred yards or so, he stopped. None of these trees showed any signs of having been pruned.

He made his way back toward the ATV, more slowly this time, eyes trained on the ground, just in case.

*Please not that.*

As he approached the trailer, his eye caught on something sticking out from the far side. Was that a foot?

He sprinted to close the distance. "Dad?"

A groan.

Spencer's heart lurched.

He jumped over the trailer's tongue.

Dad was half-sitting, half-leaning against the trailer, his hands pressed against his chest.

"Dad?" Spencer dropped to the ground next to him. "What is it?"

But he already knew. Already had his phone in his hand. Was already dialing 911.

"I'm fine—" Dad's face contorted, and he closed his eyes, his hands tightening into fists.

"You're not—" Spencer cut off as the dispatcher answered.

He had to push aside the fear gripping his own heart to speak. "I think my father's having a heart attack."

"I'm not—"

Spencer ignored him and gave the dispatcher their location, then shoved his phone into his pocket.

"Okay, Dad, we need to get you to the house. They aren't going to be able to get an ambulance back here."

"I'm not going in any ambulance." Dad sounded stronger now. "It's just indigestion. We have work to do." He pushed to his feet, and a moment of doubt hit Spencer. Was he overreacting?

But the second Dad was upright, he sagged. Spencer reached out a quick arm to help him to his feet. "You're not fine." Spencer's voice was firm. "You're getting on this ATV with me. And then you're getting into that ambulance and going to the hospital."

"Don't tell—" Dad stopped and doubled over, bracing his hands on his knees. His breath came in short gasps.

"This time I am telling you what to do, and you're going to do it." Spencer steered his father toward the ATV. "Get on."

To his relief, Dad obeyed.

Spencer climbed on and eased the ATV into gear. He wanted to push it as hard as it could go, but he wasn't sure Dad was strong enough to hold on through that.

But driving slowly gave him too much time to think. He should have recognized the signs earlier. Should have insisted that Dad take a break. Should have told Dave he couldn't help. *Should have. Should have. Should have.*

Finally, the farm's long driveway came into view. Spencer dared to throttle up a shred more. Behind him, Dad's arms went slack. His full weight slumped against Spencer.

In the distance, the wail of sirens split the air.

Spencer prayed for them to come faster.

# Chapter 3

Sophie smoothed her fingers over the translucent skin of Nana's hand.

She'd come to the hospital first thing this morning, but the nurses said Nana had been in and out because of the morphine.

So far today, she'd only been out.

Sophie had considered talking to Nana while she slept, but every time she tried, she stopped. It felt too awkward. So she'd settled for holding her hand instead. When had Nana's skin become so thin and wrinkled?

Growing up, Sophie had never thought of Nana as old. She wore jeans and kept her white hair long and burst with energy. When they'd biked together, Sophie had struggled to keep up.

But now.

Now, the skin on her face was folded into wrinkles and stained with age spots. The little hair she had was thin and stuck up in wisps around her head. Tubes and monitors ran into and out of her body.

Sophie rubbed at her eyes. As a kid, she couldn't have imagined going a week without seeing her grandma. Now, she couldn't even remember the last time she'd visited Nana. It must have been way back in undergrad. Christmas of her freshman year, maybe? Before she'd started making excuses not to come home.

How had she cut Nana completely out of her life? The woman who had taken her out on the lake every weekend as a kid when her parents were too busy signing deals to notice her. The one who had made cookies and cocoa with her on winter weekends as they sat up together late into the night. The only person she'd confided in when the boy she had a crush on in middle school liked someone else.

Nana had always been there for her.

And when Nana had needed her, when she'd been diagnosed with cancer, Sophie had been nowhere in sight. She'd been too wrapped up in her own career to call more than once or twice.

Sophie swallowed against the ache in her throat.

She needed some coffee or something. But she couldn't convince herself to leave Nana's side. What if she woke up and Sophie wasn't there? What if it was the last time she ever woke up and Sophie missed her chance to say goodbye?

Then again, the thought of going through with that goodbye made her want to run screaming from the room. Maybe it'd be better to let Nana go like this.

Sophie pushed to her feet. Mom had been right. She shouldn't have come.

She'd taken two steps toward the door when a soft sigh from behind stopped her.

She hesitated a second, indecision pulling her in two directions at once.

"Sophie?"

Hearing Nana's voice made the decision for her.

Her feet kicked into a run, adrenaline pushing her toward the elevator at the end of the hall. Ignoring the calls of the nurses behind her, she slipped through the door as it slid closed.

Inside the elevator, she heaved in a breath and jabbed blindly at the lowest button on the panel. As the elevator descended, she tried to get a grip on her emotions.

It wasn't like her to lose control like this.

Slowly, her breathing calmed. Her heart rate came back into normal range. She'd been foolish to run like that. That much she could admit. But it didn't mean she was ready to go back up there.

She wasn't sure she ever would be.

The moment the elevator doors opened, she barreled through them.

Right into someone solid.

Coffee sloshed onto the floor at her feet, and Sophie sidestepped to avoid it.

"Oh, I'm sorry, I—" But her voice failed the moment she lifted her eyes. "Sophie?"

The heart rate she'd finally gotten under control took off again. Every rational thought fled her head.

Except his name. "Spencer." It came out as an exhale.

Patches of mud caked his clothes, joined by a spreading coffee stain on his t-shirt. His hair was tousled, and his cheeks sported at least a day's worth of stubble. But somehow, he looked better than ever.

He moved a step closer, raising his arms slightly as if to give her a hug, and Sophie's stomach swooped. But half a step in, he seemed to think better of it and stepped back.

"What are you doing here?" Spencer used the crumpled napkin in his hand to wipe futilely at his shirt.

"I came to see my grandma." And had utterly failed at it. She looked away, blinking furiously. If she had to run into Spencer during this trip, it wasn't going to be while she was showing her own weakness.

"Oh, hey, it's okay." This time Spencer did pull her in for a hug.

Everything in her stiffened, then relaxed at the familiar press of his arms around her. He smelled sort of woodsy and . . . Spencer-y. She managed a shaky breath.

After a second, he cleared his throat and released her, taking a not-so-subtle step backward.

"Thanks." Sophie picked at a nonexistent piece of lint on her shirt. She couldn't look at him. If she did, it'd be too hard to remember that he wasn't part of her life anymore.

"Is your grandma okay?" Spencer's voice was guarded, yet compassionate.

Sophie shook her head, swallowing hard. "Not really. The doctors don't think it will be long." Her breath hitched. "I wanted to say goodbye, but . . ." She shook her head again. What kind of person ran out on her dying grandmother?

"But you never were good at goodbyes." Spencer said the words simply. Sophie searched his eyes but didn't find any signs of bitterness there.

"No, I guess I'm not. I just—" She didn't know how to explain it.

"I know." Spencer moved a fraction closer. "But, Soph, if you woke up tomorrow and your grandma was gone, wouldn't you regret not talking to her today? Even if it's hard."

In spite of herself, Sophie nodded. Of course Spencer was right. Then again, he'd always been way better at the emotional stuff than she was. For him, saying *I love you* had always come naturally; for her, it was a constant struggle to get the words past her lips, even though she loved him. *Did love him*, she reminded herself. *Past tense.*

Spencer gestured toward the elevator. "Come on. I'll ride up with you. I was going that way anyway."

Sophie froze. How had she been so dense? Obviously Spencer didn't just happen to be at the hospital when she needed him. For all she knew, his wife was upstairs ready to give birth to their first baby. Or their second. A lot could have happened in five years.

She forced the words out. "What are you doing here anyway?"

Spencer seemed to wilt right in front of her, and he suddenly looked exhausted. "My dad had another heart attack this morning."

Sophie inhaled sharply. "I'm sorry. Is he— I mean, will he—" Her tongue felt all tangled up. How could she ask him that?

Spencer rescued her. "He's in surgery. The doctors don't know—" He looked away and rubbed at his already tousled hair. The move was achingly familiar. It had always been his tell for when he was upset.

She laid a hand on his arm without thinking. His poor family had already been through this once.

"Anyway." Spencer pressed the button for the elevator. "If you wouldn't mind praying for him, I'd appreciate it."

"Of course." Sophie stepped into the elevator ahead of him. No sense letting him know it'd been so long since she'd prayed that God had probably forgotten who she was by now. Her prayers wouldn't do his dad much good.

The elevator door closed behind Spencer, and they rode up in silence. The weight of everything they hadn't said seemed to fill the small space, sucking out all the air.

When the doors finally opened on the third floor, Sophie's feelings were so knotted that she wasn't sure if she was relieved or disappointed.

Spencer gave her arm a gentle squeeze. "You can do this."

Sophie nodded and stepped out of the elevator. She forced her feet to carry her down the hall toward Nana's room. It took all of her willpower not to turn around for one last look at Spencer.

Finally, she couldn't resist any longer.

But when she turned back, the elevator doors were closed.

# Chapter 4

Spencer stepped off the elevator on the fourth floor, feeling like he was moving through water. Or maybe a dream.

When Sophie had walked away from him five years ago, he'd been sure that'd be the last time he'd ever see her. Seeing her again—it was surreal.

She looked almost the same—same flowing blond hair, same sleek figure, same dark, fitted business suit. But the worry in her eyes. The fear. That was new, and he'd wanted so badly to take it away. To make things better for her.

He stopped his thoughts right there. That wasn't his role anymore. He couldn't let himself go down that path again. He couldn't handle having his heart smashed by her a second time.

And based on the way his heart was acting right now, that's exactly what would happen.

Mom was still pacing the waiting room when Spencer walked back in. He knew better than to tell her to sit down. He'd already tried half a dozen times—and she'd been on her feet again within a minute each time. It was what had driven him in search of coffee. And a few minutes of peace.

Too bad he had neither to show for his trip to the lobby. Running into Sophie had only left him in more turmoil than ever.

"Any word?" He had to put his focus back on what was important. On being here for Mom. On praying for Dad. On holding their family together.

Mom shook her head, then stopped short. "What happened to you?"

"What?" Spencer followed her gaze to his shirt. "Oh. Someone bumped into me."

She nodded absently, as if she'd already forgotten her question, and resumed pacing.

"It was Sophie, actually." He'd promised himself he wouldn't say anything, but the words shot out of him anyway.

"Sophie?" Mom's voice jumped, and the slightest hint of a smile touched her eyes. "I'm so glad you asked her to come. Where is she?" She peered around him as if he might be hiding his ex-girlfriend in his back pocket.

He shook his head. "She came to see her grandma. It's—" He saw again that haunted look in her eyes as she'd told him the news. "It's near the end."

Concern furrowed Mom's forehead. "Oh, I'm sorry to hear that."

Not for the first time, Spencer marveled at his mother's compassion. Here she was, pacing a waiting room, not knowing if her husband would survive, and she was worried about someone else. Not just anyone else, but the woman who had walked away from him, who had never been willing to meet his family, let alone become part of it.

"Tell her I'll keep her family in my prayers." Mom pressed a hand to her heart.

Spencer eyed Mom. Tell her? When did she think he was going to see Sophie again? "Mom, I'm not—"

She lifted a finger in warning. He may be an adult, but the gesture still had the power to silence him. "Since the moment you two broke up, I've told you God has his ways of bringing people together when the time is right."

"I wouldn't start planning the wedding just yet," Spencer said dryly. He believed in God's power as much as the next person, but he was pretty sure that wasn't what was at play here. It was just a coincidence. One that would pass over soon enough. Until then, he'd just have to do his best to avoid Sophie.

And to keep Mom from getting her hopes up.

"Tyler hasn't called yet?" A stab of guilt jabbed him at the cheap tactic to change the subject. But it worked.

Mom's face fell. "He's busy. I'm sure he'll be here soon."

Spencer held back his snort. When his brother had taken off ten years ago, he'd made it clear he had no intention of ever returning. Hadn't bothered to visit for even a day last time Dad was in the hospital. As usual, he'd left everything to Spencer to take care of.

If they were really lucky this time, Tyler would call to send his love.

Love, his foot. In Spencer's book, love meant being there for people.

A weight pressed on his chest. Who was he to talk? Dad had always been there for him. But where had he been when Dad needed him this morning?

"Mom?" His voice came out scratchy. "I'm sorry."

She paused and really looked at him, then crossed the room and had her arms around him in a second flat. Her head only came halfway up his chest, but that didn't matter. He felt safe here.

"This is not your fault." Her voice was firm and sure.

He nodded. But that didn't stop the tears that dripped from his chin into her hair.

Sophie had been standing outside Nana's room for ten minutes, trying to work up the courage to step over the threshold. It felt like taking that step would mark a turning point in her life—one she wasn't sure she was ready for.

But Spencer was right. She'd never be able to live with herself if she didn't say goodbye. Even if it was the hardest thing she'd ever had to do.

She pulled in a quick breath and stepped into the room, her heels clicking against the floor tiles.

"Nana?" She sounded like a little girl who wasn't sure if she was in trouble. Which was exactly how she felt.

Nana's eyes had been closed, but she opened them and turned her head toward the door. Her smile made the wrinkles on her face stand into ridges. Sophie moved closer to the bed and took Nana's outstretched hand.

"I'm glad you came back."

Sophie sniffed and dropped her gaze to the floor. "I'm sorry about before."

But Nana pulled her closer and smoothed a hand over her cheek. Sophie closed her eyes. She was supposed to be here to comfort Nana, and here Nana was the one offering comfort, just as she always had.

"No worries, my Sophie. This is easier for me than it is for you."

Sophie gave a weak laugh. Somehow, she didn't think dying was the easier option.

Nana grimaced as she shifted in the bed.

"You're uncomfortable. Do you need more morphine?" Sophie reached for the button the nurses had showed her and held it out to Nana.

"Not right now. I want to be awake to talk to my Sophie. Anyway, I can handle a little pain in my life. Soon I'll be going where there's no more pain." She said it matter-of-factly, as if she were commenting on the weather.

Sophie winced. "Please don't talk like that, Nana."

"And why not, dear? You don't want me to go to heaven?" Nana's eyes held that glint they always took on when she was teasing.

But it wasn't funny. "Not yet, no."

Nana let out a half-laugh, half-cough. "That's my Sophie. Same stubborn tone you used to give me when I told you to go to bed and you wanted to stay up. It didn't work then, and it's not going to work now. I'm ready to go home to heaven, and whenever Jesus is ready to call me, there's nothing you can do about it, so you might as well accept it."

Sophie gazed toward the window, unwilling to meet Nana's eyes. She didn't accept it. Not by a long shot. But it was better to appease her grandma, just like she'd done as a kid, going into her room but lying up reading for hours into the night.

Nana patted her hand. "Tell me about your life in Chicago."

Sophie breathed easier. This, at least, was a safe topic. "I'm at Heartland, one of the biggest real estate developers in the country. I'm on track to become VP in record time."

Nana waved a hand through the air. "I'm proud of you for that. But I didn't ask about your job. I asked about your *life*. What do you do with yourself when you're not working?"

Sophie shrugged. "Not much. I'm pretty much working all the time."

Nana's wrinkles deepened. "Are you happy?"

Sophie was ready to toss off a flippant yes. Of course she was happy. She had a prestigious job, an apartment to die for, everything she'd worked so hard to achieve since she was a little girl.

But that empty feeling from last night pressed on her chest. She pushed it away. "Don't worry, Nana. I'm happy."

She ignored the niggling doubt that squirmed into her thoughts.

Nana's gaze cut through her. "Don't forget that life isn't all about achievements. They're nice in their way. But they're never going to fill you up. They'll never replace love. Don't go through life alone, Sophie. You'll miss so much."

Sophie shifted in her seat. Nana was wrong. Being alone was the only way to guarantee you never disappointed anyone. Never failed to live up to their expectations.

"I'm fine, Nana," she finally said.

Nana gave her a hard look. "Good. But just in case you need a reminder, I want you to have this." She slid the amethyst ring from her left hand and held it out to Sophie.

But Sophie shook her head and lifted her hands, as if fending it off. "No, Nana. I couldn't." That ring was as much a part of Nana as her hair or her voice. Sophie couldn't remember ever seeing her without it.

Nana thrust the ring closer. "I'm not going to need this where I'm going. It'd make me happy to know you had it."

Sophie's hands fell. How could she resist that? She reluctantly slid the ring onto her finger. The stone seemed to pull in and give off light at the same time.

"Did I ever tell you about that ring?" Nana closed her eyes and shifted against her pillow, letting out a soft moan.

"Can I get you anything?" Sophie's heart twisted to see Nana suffering. She picked up the morphine button and held it out, but Nana waved it off.

"It was from your grandfather. The ring."

Sophie held her breath. Her grandfather had died long before she was born, and Nana almost never spoke about him.

"He didn't have money for a wedding ring when we were first married, but he bought that for me a few years later. He called it a forever ring." The creases of pain around her lips were replaced by a soft smile. "I was so mad at him for so long. He promised me forever, but then he left me a few years later."

"But—"

Nana lifted a feeble hand. "It wasn't his choice. I know that. But when you're grieving, nothing makes much sense."

Sophie nodded. That's how she felt already, and Nana was still here with her.

"I don't think I handled my grief very well. Especially with your mother. She wanted to talk about her father, but it hurt me too much, so I didn't let her. And then after Jordan—"

Sophie choked on a sharp gasp at her older brother's name, but Nana kept talking as if she hadn't noticed. "I didn't talk to her about that, either. And I watched as she shut her heart down." She clutched at Sophie's hand. "I don't want that for you."

"I'm not— I won't—" But shutting down her heart. That was the only way she'd survived so far. Was the only way she'd survive Nana's death, too.

"Anyway." Nana released her grip. "Now I get to go home and see them." She closed her eyes, and her hand fell limp. Sophie's heart clambered up her throat. Surely she didn't mean this moment? Holding her breath, she leaned toward her grandmother.

Nana's eyes sprang open, and Sophie jumped back, pressing a hand to her chest.

*Thank goodness.*

"Promise me—" Nana wrapped Sophie's hands in both of hers. "Whenever you look at that ring, you remember that forever is real. Not here. But after, in heaven. And you keep your heart open. To God. And to the people he puts into your life to love you. For however long they're part of it."

Sophie stared at her smooth hands planted in Nana's wrinkled ones. "I promise."

It was a promise she was pretty sure she couldn't keep. But she'd try. For Nana's sake.

Nana closed her eyes again, and Sophie sat watching her, trying to memorize every feature. After a few minutes, Nana spoke again. "I'm glad you found your way home, Sophie."

Sophie nodded, her throat too full to answer.

She may be home, but she felt more lost than ever.

# Chapter 5

Spencer swiped at the sweat on his brow. He'd been pruning like mad all morning, trying to outrun the images of Sophie that insisted on pushing into his thoughts. The way she tipped her chin up when she laughed. The way her hand had always fit perfectly in his. The way she was just the right height that when he wrapped his arms around her, he could rest his chin on her head.

*Stop.*

He gave the pruning saw another thrust. It'd taken him years to stop thinking about Sophie every day. And seeing her for only a few minutes yesterday had undone all of that.

Spencer clipped one last branch, then stood back to survey the orchard. A ragged sigh escaped him. There were so many trees left. And who knew how long Dad would be out of commission. Which meant it was all up to him. Again.

Much as he loved the farm, the weight of its responsibility pressed on him right now. How would his life have been different if he'd been like Tyler and left and never come back? Would he and Sophie still be together? Married?

Spencer scrubbed at his face. He couldn't go down this what-if road. He'd made his choice—and Sophie had made hers.

His phone pealed, and he tore it out of his pocket, inexplicably hoping his thoughts of Sophie had conjured a call from her. Which was ridiculous. She'd probably already left town. The Sophie he'd known wouldn't have stuck around any longer than necessary, especially not when things got emotional.

He grimaced as he caught the number on the phone. "About time."

"How is he?" Tyler's voice was raw and cracked.

"So you do care?" The words were out before Spencer could stop himself.

"Don't be a jerk." But Tyler's voice lacked the older-brother authority Spencer was used to hearing from him.

"That's rich. You're the one who waited nearly twenty-four hours to even bother to call, and I'm the jerk?" Spencer bent to stack the branches he'd cut, jamming his phone between his shoulder and his ear.

"Knock it off, Spence. Is Dad okay?"

Spencer relented. He'd never heard his brother plead like that before. "He was in surgery most of the day yesterday. They said two of his arteries were almost completely blocked. They put in stents, but—" He really didn't want to deliver this kind of news over the phone.

"But?" Tyler's voice was hoarse.

"His heart was pretty damaged. If he has another heart attack . . ." Did he really have to say this? "They're not sure what the outcome would be." The words left a bitter taste in his mouth.

Spencer waited. This was the part where Tyler would say he sent his love and then hang up.

"Do you think—" Tyler broke off as a small voice started to wail in the background. The phone rustled, and Spencer caught the low murmur of Tyler talking to someone on the other end. The words were too quiet to catch.

After a moment, the wailing stopped. "Sorry." Tyler sounded as weary as Spencer felt. "The boys won't stop crying for Julia."

Spencer tried to picture his twin nephews, but he'd only seen a picture of them in last year's Christmas card—two chubby toddlers with Tyler's bright blue eyes and Julia's dark hair.

"Julia working today?"

Tyler was silent so long that Spencer pulled his phone away from his ear to make sure the call hadn't dropped.

"Tyler, you there?"

"Yeah." That raw edge had returned to his voice. "Julia's not—" Tyler's voice broke. "She left."

Spencer dropped the bundle of branches he'd been hauling.

"What do you mean she left?" Spencer had always thought of Tyler and Julia as the definition of soul mates—same interests, same taste in music, even the same corny sense of humor.

"She packed a bag, took one of the credit cards, and walked out the door."

"When?"

"Yesterday. I spent the day trying to get her to stay and then trying to figure out how to make the boys stop crying. I didn't realize my phone had died, otherwise . . ."

Spencer rubbed at his forehead. He'd assumed the worst of his brother. And here Tyler had been going through his own crisis. "I'm sorry, Ty." What else could he say? "Maybe she'll come back."

"She won't." Tyler's voice was dull. "There's someone else."

A white heat surged through Spencer. He and Tyler may not be close anymore, but once upon a time, they'd been each other's staunchest defenders, and that instinct came rushing back now.

"I mean, I have no idea how to take care of two boys on my own." Tyler's voice went up. "Julia was the one who was good at that. How am I supposed to—"

"Look, why don't you and the boys come to visit. Mom and Dad have been dying to meet their grandsons." He winced at the word choice, but it was too late to change it.

"You think they would want to see me after—" Tyler's swallow sounded through the phone.

"I know they do. Kind of annoying how much they want to see you, actually, considering I'm right here." Spencer tried to play it off as a joke, but the truth was, he'd always felt a little bit like the older brother in the parable of the prodigal son.

"Yeah. Maybe." High-pitched cries cut through the background. "Jonah, no." Tyler's exasperated yell made Spencer smile. He'd wondered what kind of father Tyler made.

His brother came back on the line. "I gotta go. Jonah got into the markers."

The line went dead, and Spencer lowered the phone slowly. That was not at all how he'd expected that conversation to go.

He restacked his dropped bundle of branches.

If Julia could leave Tyler after six years of marriage, what guarantee did anyone have that love could be forever?

Apparently there was none.

In which case, maybe it was best Sophie had left him when she did—think how much worse it would have hurt if they'd already built a life together.

৻৴৵৹

Sophie bent over the rows of colorful tulips that bobbed in the early morning sun. With deft movements, she snipped flowers here and there, careful to spread out her selections as their gardener Alex had taught her years ago.

The garden had always been her favorite place on the entire property. She'd spent hours crawling around in the dirt out here, until Mom had told her she was too old to go around with ragged nails and dirt-stained knuckles.

But being out here, savoring the rustle of the breeze in her hair, the soft baking of the sun on her back—it almost made her, not happy, exactly, but at peace with being home.

A song Nana used to sing popped into her head, and she hummed the tune as she clipped. She couldn't remember all the words, but she thought it had something to do with "Savior's arms."

But thinking of arms made her think of Spencer's arms. Of the flippy thing her stomach had done when he wrapped them around her. Force of habit, certainly, but it had been disconcerting nonetheless. And nice. She couldn't deny that.

But she had to.

She shoved the thought away and straightened, cutting off her humming mid-song.

She carried her armful of flowers into the house and surveyed the collection of ornate vases Alex would fill with fresh flowers throughout the summer. She reached past them to grab a simple, straight one that was more to Nana's style. On a whim, she grabbed a second one just like it and placed half the bouquet in each.

All the way to the hospital, she debated with herself.

Bringing flowers to Spencer's father would probably mean running into Spencer again. And she should be doing everything possible to avoid him—it would be better for both of them that way.

But she couldn't pretend she didn't want to see him again.

Badly.

By the time she got to the hospital, her mind was made up.

She strode to the information desk and asked for the room number for Marcus Weston.

"I'm not seeing . . ." The man trailed off, typing again.

A sudden fear clutched at her stomach. What if he hadn't made it? Her pulse quickened as the volunteer at the desk typed something into the computer and scanned the screen, then typed some more.

She should have stayed with Spencer. Should have been there for him. Shouldn't have let him go through this alone.

"Ah, there he is." The volunteer scribbled on a slip of paper as Sophie leaned heavily into the counter. Her hand shook as she took the paper from him.

"Thank you," she managed to get out as she grabbed the vases and spun away from the desk.

She navigated to room 421.

The door was slightly ajar, but she didn't feel right just walking in, so she tapped softly on the frame.

"Come in," a woman's voice called a moment later.

Sophie pressed hesitantly on the door and stepped inside. Unlike Nana's private room, this room had two beds. The far bed held a man who must be closer to Nana's age, judging from the silver wisps and wrinkles. In the closer bed, a man with the same broad forehead and defined jaw as Spencer was half-propped, talking to a petite woman perched on the edge of the bed.

Sophie stepped into the room, her heels sounding too loud on the tile floor. She stopped halfway to the bed. "I'm looking for Mr. Weston." She sounded like a timid child rather than the fiery developer who had left grown contractors quaking for missing a deadline.

"You found him." The man even sounded like Spencer, though his voice was a touch deeper. "What can I do for you?"

Sophie laughed, the man managing to put her instantly at ease. "Absolutely nothing. Actually, I stopped by to give you these."

She held one of the vases of tulips out, and Mrs. Weston took it from her, her eyebrows raised at her husband.

"Well, now, you're going to get me in trouble with my wife." Mr. Weston winked at her. "She doesn't like when I get flowers from pretty young ladies."

Mrs. Weston snorted. "I'm not worried." But she set the flowers on the side table, then leaned down to kiss the top of her husband's head.

Something in Sophie jumped, and she averted her eyes. She didn't want to intrude on their tender moment.

"Not that I don't enjoy getting flowers from mysterious strangers," Mr. Weston said. "But maybe you'd like to tell me your name so I know who to thank."

Sophie felt her cheeks warm. She hadn't even introduced herself.

"I'm sorry. I'm Sophie Olsen. Spencer and I—" She caught herself.

"Oh, Sophie." Spencer's mother jumped to her feet and wrapped her in an unexpected hug. "It's so nice to meet you at last. Spencer mentioned that he'd run into you yesterday. I added you and your grandmother to my prayers last night."

"Thank you." Sophie's arms circled the woman tentatively, and her head spun. Spencer had wanted her to meet his parents so many times, but she'd always resisted. Which apparently hadn't stopped him from telling them about her. So why was this woman greeting her so kindly?

"Is Spencer, um— I mean, did he step out for a coffee again?" Sophie felt ridiculous asking, but her desire to see him was stronger than her embarrassment.

"No, he had some work to do on the farm. Boy never stops working," Mr. Weston said. "Trying to chase off demons, if you ask me. Not that

I'm complaining. He keeps that place running." Pride laced his every word about his son.

A pang hit Sophie right in the center of her chest. What would it be like to hear her parents talk about her like that?

"I wouldn't think you'd complain." Spencer's mom poured water into a plastic cup and passed it to her husband. "If he hadn't had the sense to call 911 when you said you were fine, you wouldn't be here today." She turned to Sophie. "Men tend to let their pride get in the way of their common sense sometimes, if you haven't noticed."

Sophie suspected she was talking about more than her husband, but she let it pass.

"You should go out to the farm," Mr. Weston said. "I'm sure he could use a break."

"Oh, I'm sure he's busy." Sophie rubbed a petal of one of the tulips. "Anyway, I should get to my grandma. Just tell him—" Just tell him what? That she wanted to see him? The full extent of how ridiculous she'd been to come searching for him hit her.

His life was here.

Hers was in Chicago.

"Just tell him I said goodbye."

# Chapter 6

The sun was low in the sky, casting a kaleidoscope of colors onto Lake Michigan, by the time Sophie left the hospital. Although Nana had slept through most of the afternoon, it had been comforting just to be near her.

But sitting all day had left her with pent-up energy she needed to burn off. The thought of going back to her parents' wasn't exactly appealing. She wished for the hundredth time that her parents had a relationship more like that of Spencer's parents. Sitting in Nana's room with nothing to do but think, her mind kept drifting to the way Mrs. Weston had kissed her husband and poured him a glass of water before he even asked for one. No wonder Spencer had believed in true love. He apparently had a view of it every day. But Sophie knew better. Even if a couple seemed to be in love, all of that could change in a single, devastating moment.

But still, the way Spencer's parents had looked at each other—she couldn't shake that image. Only two people in her life had ever looked at her like that. One of them was dying.

But the other—he was right down the road.

Sophie chewed her lip. She couldn't do this again. But maybe Spencer's dad was right. Maybe Spencer did need a break. He'd always been a workaholic. More so when he was worried. And he didn't worry about anything more than he did his family.

Before she could second-guess herself, she directed her car toward Hidden Blossom Farms. She'd driven past it a hundred times in her life. But she'd never so much as turned down the driveway. Hadn't even known Spencer, who'd gone to school in the next town over, lived there until he was assigned as her friend Cade's roommate in college.

But today, this moment, she felt almost compelled to see it. To see the life she'd said no to when she'd walked away from Spencer. To convince herself she'd done the right thing in leaving him.

The big farmhouse near the road was dark, but warm light spilled from the open garage door of a large pole shed near the end of the driveway. Hesitating only a second, Sophie pressed her foot to the gas. She'd come this far already.

As she pulled to a stop in front of the shed, her eyes picked out a modest ranch home beyond it. Through the twilight, she could just see the large open meadow behind the house. Early season wildflowers added a spark of color against the darkening grass.

Sophie's heels sank into the soft gravel as soon as she stepped out of the car, but she picked her way to the shed door.

Blinking against the bright lights inside, she peered around the large space. A tractor and an assortment of what Sophie assumed was farming equipment filled one half of the shed. But the other half was set up as a woodworking shop. Several large tools dominated the space: what she thought was a table saw and a workbench covered with buckets of paint and stain. But her eyes slipped past the rest of the tools to the finished products scattered around the space. There was a rocking chair with gracefully curved arms, an elegant console table, and—

Sophie's breath caught, and she moved into the shed as if pulled.

When she reached it, she stopped. The seat was covered with boxes, and a dirty towel hung over the back, but she recognized it.

The bench was a perfect replica of the one in the park where Spencer had proposed to her.

She ran her fingers across the wood and let the memories submerge her. They'd talked on that park bench. Laughed on that bench. Kissed on that bench.

"Hey, there."

Sophie jumped and yanked her hand off the bench. Her face flamed and her heart set up a staccato rhythm as she whirled to catch Spencer watching her. How long had he been standing there?

"Sorry, I—" She felt as if she'd been caught prying into his private life. "This is beautiful." She touched the bench one last time, then shuffled away from it.

"Thanks." Spencer tilted his head, staring at her as if he'd never seen her before.

He looked at home here in his worn jeans and faded flannel. Even the scruff on his chin seemed to belong in these rugged surroundings.

She glanced down at her tailored navy pants suit. She, on the other hand, did not belong.

"What are you doing here, Soph?" Spencer's voice was gentle but guarded.

Sophie stared at him. She had completely forgotten why she'd thought it would be a good idea to come.

"I just—" She licked her dry lips. "I just wanted to thank you."

He raised his eyebrows. "Thank me?"

"For talking me into not running away from seeing my grandma yesterday. You were right."

"You're welcome." Spencer shuffled his feet. An awkward silence fell.

Finally, Spencer sighed. "Was there anything else you needed?" She hated the formality in his tone, as if he didn't know her better than anyone else in the world.

What had she been thinking, coming here? Of course he didn't want to see her. "Nothing else." She tried to apply the same detachment to her voice and found with relief that it was easier than she'd expected. She picked her way across the shed toward the door.

She paused when she was even with him. "Bye, Spencer." The words fell from her lips and hovered in the air between them.

Jaw tight, he nodded. She waited another beat, then continued toward her car, pushing down the sting at the back of her throat. She was being ridiculous and overly emotional after her day with Nana. What had she expected? That he'd pull her into his arms and say he'd missed her and couldn't live without her? It's not like she wanted that.

"Soph?"

She froze, gripping the car door, an unexpected hope tugging at a place deep in her heart.

"Yeah?" She couldn't look at him. Couldn't bear to have that hope punctured. Not today.

"Do you want some dinner?"

# Chapter 7

He was the biggest fool on the planet. Spencer knew that with certainty the moment the words were out of his mouth.

But a warmth he hadn't felt in years spread through him as he watched Sophie turn toward him, the moonlight spinning her hair into a river of light. He was seized with the urge to gather her in his arms and run his fingers through it.

*Yep, definitely an idiot.*

He was only setting himself up for heartbreak. And the worst part was, he didn't care.

"Dinner sounds nice." Sophie smiled. He'd missed that smile. The way the left side of her mouth lifted a fraction higher than the right.

"I was going to order in pizza tonight, but—" He eyed her sharp suit. She was used to better than Jerry's Pizza. "We can do something else, if you want."

"Pizza sounds great." She started toward him, but her heel snagged on a rock, and she stumbled. He lunged forward just in time to grab her before she face-planted.

As soon as she was steady on her feet, he snatched his hands back and shoved them into his pockets.

"Thanks." Sophie sounded breathless.

He took stock of her three-inch heels. "You're never going to make it across the yard in those. It's a swamp from all the rain."

Sophie glanced from the yard to her heels, then kicked off her shoes, standing on the gravel in her bare feet. "There."

Spencer's mouth fell open as she stooped to retrieve her shoes. He'd only ever seen hints of this spontaneous version of Sophie.

But she winced as she took one step and then another.

Before he could think what he was doing, Spencer positioned himself with his back to her. "Hop on."

She gave a disbelieving laugh. "I'm not going to ride on your back."

"Seriously, Soph, just get on." It's not like it'd be the first time he'd given her a piggyback ride.

"Seriously, Spencer, no."

"Suit yourself." Good to know her stubborn streak hadn't changed. He walked purposefully toward the house. Behind him, he heard Sophie's sharp inhales with every step. But he kept going. Two could play the stubborn game.

By the time he'd crossed the yard and reached the front door, she was only halfway across the driveway. She eyed her shoes.

"Don't put those on," Spencer called. "You'll break an ankle."

Sophie's exasperated huff made him chuckle. "You sure you don't want a piggyback ride? Last offer."

The moonlight played over her features, and Spencer could pick out the moment her hesitation gave way to resignation. He jogged back across the yard, ignoring the squish of water in his shoes from the saturated grass.

When he reached her, he gave a slight bow. "M'lady. Your chariot."

She rolled her eyes, but a smile tugged her lips up.

He let his own lips tip into a grin, then turned and stood braced for her to climb onto his back.

He tensed as her hands fell on his shoulders. Oh yeah, this had been a big mistake. But he couldn't exactly dump her back onto the ground now.

Gritting his teeth and willing himself not to notice the feel of her against him, he charged across the yard. She gasped and tightened her grip around his neck.

The moment they made it to the porch, he deposited her on the bottom step. Working hard to keep from brushing against her, he reached around her to open the door and gestured for her to enter in front of him. Once she was inside, he took a moment to collect his thoughts before he lost his mind altogether.

"I'll call for pizza." He pulled out his phone and dialed as she wandered around his living room, pausing now and then to look at a photo. He'd always considered his home comfortable, but now he saw it through her eyes: the well-worn couch and faded curtains. The anything-but-elegant wooden coffee table he'd made as a kid—one of his first woodworking projects. The lamp he'd found on the side of the road and rewired.

Was she thinking about how she'd escaped a life so beneath her standards when she walked away from him?

He finished placing the order and hung up the phone, then immediately wished he hadn't. Now what were they going to do? What did you talk about with the woman who'd shredded your heart five years ago?

*Probably not that.*

"You have a nice place." Sophie settled into his favorite easy chair. "It's so cozy."

Spencer laughed a little. Sophie had always been diplomatic. "Thanks."

He sat at the end of the couch farthest from her chair. That way he couldn't do anything stupid. Like act on his impulse to grab her hand.

"So how long are you in town?" There. That should put a damper on his thoughts. Bring him back to reality.

Sophie's sigh was weighted. "I don't know. My boss wants me back as soon as possible. But—" She chewed her lip as she'd always done when she was uncertain. "I feel like it's important to stay with Nana until the end. I know it won't make a difference, but—"

Spencer shifted a fraction toward her. "It *will* make a difference."

Her eyes held his. "You think so?"

He nodded. "Having people you love around you for those life-changing moments? That's important."

Sophie's lips parted.

There were so many things he could say right now. So many things he shouldn't say.

Spencer jumped to his feet. "Drinks! You want something to drink?"

Sophie startled at his abrupt movement, but he needed to put at least one wall between them for a minute.

He was already on his way to the kitchen. "I have water, soda, milk. I don't think I have any wine, but—"

"Water is good."

"Water it is then." In the kitchen, Spencer braced his arms against the counter and took a few slow breaths. He had to get himself together. He was catching up with an old friend. That was all.

His feelings in check, he pushed off the counter and grabbed two glasses out of the cupboard.

"So," he called toward the living room as he grabbed the water jug out of the fridge, "where are you these days?" How strange that he didn't know where she lived, let alone what her life was like. Or if she was with someone.

The sucker punch of the thought drew him up short, and he jerked his arm. Water cascaded onto the counter.

"Shoot!" He yanked the jug upright.

"Everything okay in there?" Sophie's voice drifted into the room.

"Fine. Just a little spill." He gritted his teeth as he yanked a towel out of the drawer and sopped up the mess.

"Here, let me help." Sophie glided into the room, still barefoot, and moved the water glasses to a dry spot on the counter. She reached past him to grab the jug. Her arm grazed the hairs on his, and he shifted away.

"I still live in Chicago." She took the towel from him and wiped the outside of the glasses, then passed him one.

He took a long drink, watching her over the top of his glass. Did she always have to be so self-assured and in control? Wasn't her heart bouncing all over the place the way his was? Then again, there was no reason for it to be. She clearly adored her new life.

"And what do you do there?" Whatever it was, he had no doubt she'd made a success of it. She'd never known how to fail.

"I work for a real estate development firm. On my way to VP, actually."

Spencer's grip tightened on his glass. "That's great, Soph." He was happy she was successful, but there was no love lost between him and real estate developers. The parasites came sniffing after his parents' farm every few years, looking for an opportunity to snatch it up.

Before he could think of something else to say, the doorbell rang. He escaped to grab the pizza.

When he returned, Sophie had the table set with plates she must have rummaged through the kitchen to find. It warmed him from the inside to think of her making herself at home here.

*You are being a supreme idiot.*

She had just told him she lived in Chicago. That she was happy there. Making herself at home here was the farthest thing from her mind.

He held the pizza box out to her as he slid into the chair across from her. He grabbed his own slice and set it on his plate before folding his hands and bowing his head. Across from him, he heard Sophie shuffle a napkin and sigh. He peeked up without raising his head, just in time to see her fold her hands, too. His mind went blank. He and Sophie had prayed over their meals together so many times, but it suddenly felt too intimate.

"Thank you for this food, Lord," he finally managed. "And thank you for old—" His mind scrambled for a safe word. "For old friends."

"Amen," Sophie murmured.

"Amen." He grabbed his water glass and guzzled down half its contents in one gulp.

When he lowered the glass, he dove into his pizza. It'd been a long day, and he was famished. And if his mouth was full, he would have an excuse not to talk. Not to say something stupid.

He was grabbing another piece when Sophie finally broke the silence. "Tell me about the farm."

Spencer stopped with the pizza slice halfway to his mouth. In the three years they'd been together, Sophie had never once asked about the farm.

"What do you want to know?"

She dabbed at her lips with a napkin, looking thoughtful. "How long has it been in your family?"

He did some quick math. "About a hundred and twenty years? My great-great grandfather planted a small cherry orchard, and each generation has expanded it over the years. We have about fifty acres now, with a few thousand trees."

"That's— Wow." Sophie sat back in her chair, laying her napkin on her plate. "That's a lot."

His face warmed. If he didn't know better, he'd think she was impressed.

He pushed back his chair. "The cherries should be in bloom in a day or two. You should come see them. They're pretty spectacular."

Great. Now he was inviting rejection.

But that smile lit her face again. "I'd like that."

He carried their plates to the dishwasher, avoiding her eyes. Did she even know what she was doing to him?

"What about the woodworking?" She stood and brought their empty glasses to him.

He lifted a shoulder. "Just a side gig I do in the winter when things are slower on the farm. Brings in a little extra income." Income they desperately needed after last year's failed crop. Which was why he had so many half-completed projects in the shop. He'd taken on way more than he could handle this winter to try to make ends meet.

"You're very talented, Spencer." Sophie kept her gaze directed at the dishwasher, but her cheeks pinked.

Her comment pleased him more than it should. He slammed the dishwasher closed harder than he meant to. "Thanks."

He turned to make his escape to a less confined room, but she was right there.

She took a step back to avoid getting run over.

"I should get going." But she didn't move. Something hovered in her words, and for a moment Spencer let himself think she wanted him to ask her to stay.

He dried his hands on his pants. "Yeah. I'll walk you out."

⚬⚬⚬

Sophie could feel Spencer's presence behind her as he shepherded her to the door. Dinner had been nice. Better than nice, actually. It'd been the best night she'd had in a long time.

Which was why she had to get out of here.

Sooner rather than later.

She scooped up her shoes from the rug in front of the door, then let Spencer reach past her to open it. Still a gentleman.

"You should visit Violet while you're back." Spencer followed her onto the porch.

She froze. "I don't think she'd want to see me." If Sophie had one regret about how she'd handled things after she and Spencer broke up, it was cutting her best friend out of her life. But at the time, it had seemed easiest to cut every last tie to Hope Springs. She hadn't come back for Violet and Cade's wedding. Or for Cade's funeral two years ago. The memory of the text from her mom saying Cade had died slammed into her. She and Vi and Cade had been a trio since grade school. Cade was like a brother to her. And the thought that he was gone—it had been too much to deal with. She couldn't face saying goodbye to him. Couldn't face seeing Vi's grief.

So she'd sent a card and told herself it would be enough. And then she'd buried herself even deeper in her work.

"She'd want to see you." Spencer's eyes were too gentle, too understanding.

"How is she?" Sophie managed to keep her voice steady, not to betray the roil of emotions churning in her stomach at the thought of what her friend had gone through without her. Of course, that didn't mean Spencer couldn't see them.

He reached for her arm but dropped his hand before it made contact. "She's doing okay, I guess. She and Cade had an antique store that she's kept going. But she's not the same person she used to be." He gripped the porch railing but turned his head toward her. "Losing someone does that to a person."

The moment Sophie's eyes landed on his, lined in silver in the moonlight, they skipped away. What she saw in his—that wasn't something she was prepared to deal with.

"Thanks for tonight." She rushed down the steps, ignoring the cold sting of the concrete on her bare feet, the cold squish of the mud between her toes as she stepped into the grass.

By the time she'd reached the driveway, her feet were so numb she barely felt the stab of the jagged rocks. Too bad the ache in her heart wasn't as easily dimmed.

# Chapter 8

Sophie stared down the doors of the church as a warm breeze lifted the hair off her neck. Her parents had already gone inside, but she couldn't quite bring herself to step through the doors. The relentless pounding of the Lake Michigan surf below seemed to take the place of her heartbeat. She didn't know what she was doing here. Not really.

She hadn't been inside a church anywhere in years. But Nana had barely woken at all yesterday, and she felt out of options. Maybe if she put in some time at church, God would listen to her prayers.

Anyway, in one of Nana's few lucid moments, she'd made Sophie promise to come.

Sophie steeled her shoulders. If she could face angry contractors and disgruntled buyers, she could handle an hour of church.

She pulled the door open and strode inside, letting her eyes travel the space. She hadn't been in here since her senior year of high school. And yet so little had changed. To the left was the same oversize fireplace surrounded by several leather couches. Above, the same high, white wooden beams gave the room an open, airy feel. Scattered groups of people talked and laughed together. Everyone seemed so at home here. Had she really felt that way once, too?

She tried to wind her way through the clusters of people without drawing attention to herself.

But just before she reached the entrance to the sanctuary, she lifted her eyes, and they fell on Spencer. She stopped abruptly, barely noticing when someone ran into her from behind.

"Sorry," she mumbled. But her eyes were locked on Spencer's, and she couldn't tear them away, no matter how much she wanted to.

She'd spent most of the day yesterday convincing herself that the things she'd felt the other night at his house were only nostalgia—a reminder of the time before there were careers and apartments and dying grandmothers to worry about.

But with his eyes on her, the strength of her arguments crumbled at her feet.

Spencer's expression remained neutral, but he waved her over.

It was only then that she noticed the others standing around him. A couple who looked vaguely familiar and two women, one of whom Sophie recognized immediately, even from the back. Those dark curls could only belong to her former best friend.

Her heart jumped as Vi spotted her, gave her a gigantic smile, and broke away from the group to charge across the lobby. She threw her arms around Sophie and engulfed her in a hug that left Sophie gasping for air.

Sophie clung to her former best friend, even as she scrunched her eyes against the wave of emotion.

"Spencer said you were back. It's so good to see you." Vi was still squeezing her tight.

"You, too." Sophie's voice was too full. She didn't deserve a welcome like this. Not after she'd abandoned the one person she'd promised to be there for forever.

She pulled back, gripping her friend's shoulders. "I'm so sorry about Cade."

Vi nodded and blinked a few times. Her eyes lacked the bright spark and easy smile that had led her to be voted "friendliest senior" in high school. "Thanks, I—"

But the rest of the group reached them. Vi gestured to the couple that Sophie thought she knew but couldn't place. "Soph, do you remember Ethan and Ariana? They graduated a year ahead of us." The couple unwound their arms from around each other and each held out a hand to Sophie. Now that Vi said their names, she recognized them. Ethan had always been a star athlete, but his whole family had been killed in an accident. Sophie always wondered how someone recovered from something like that. It was hard enough to lose one person.

"And this is Emma." Violet gestured to a tall, pretty blond standing close to Spencer.

Very close.

The woman scrutinized her with a hard look but held out a hand.

Sophie forced her hand forward even as her shoulders tensed. Her eyes shot to the woman's left hand. Ring free.

*Not that it matters.*

"And, of course, you know Spencer." What was that look Vi gave her? Could she read the swirl of Sophie's thoughts at seeing her ex with another woman?

Spencer offered a tight smile.

"I didn't know you came to church here." Sophie directed her words to Spencer. "I thought you always went over in Silver Bay." It'd been the only reason she'd even considered coming here this morning.

"We started coming here to be with Vi after Cade's death." The blond woman—Emma—answered for him.

Sophie nodded stiffly.

Of course they had. They'd been here for Vi when she hadn't.

Ethan glanced at his watch, then fiddled with a pager on his hip. "We should probably go grab a seat."

Sophie scanned the nearly empty lobby. Her parents had probably long since taken their customary spot in the second row from the front.

Vi nudged her. "Sit with us?"

Sitting with Spencer and his new girlfriend for an hour sounded like absolutely the last thing Sophie wanted to do. But the church was full, and she didn't exactly feel like parading to the front to join her parents.

She followed the group as they filed into a half-full row near the back. Her whole body tensed as she realized she'd be sandwiched right between Vi and Spencer. She squeezed as close to Vi as she could in the cramped space and bowed her head, trying to recall the words of the prayers Nana had taught her as a little girl, but her mind drew a blank.

Panic welled low in her stomach. Had it really been that long since she'd prayed? What right did she even have to be here?

Her legs itched with the need to get away. But she'd have to climb over Spencer and Emma to escape, and she wasn't about to attempt that. She tried to direct her attention to Pastor Zelner. But she was too aware of every shift in Spencer's position, every accidental brush of his arm against hers. His familiar scent of spicy woodland and warm cinnamon wafted over her.

By the time church was over, Sophie was ready to bolt.

"It was so nice to see you again." She leaned over to hug Vi, then pushed to her feet.

"Wait. Where do you think you're going?" Vi latched onto her arm, as if afraid she'd sneak away. "We always grab some lunch after church. You have to come."

Sophie scanned the church, searching for her parents. They were standing on opposite sides of the sanctuary, each deep in conversation. Hopefully they wouldn't be long.

"Sorry, Vi. I'd love to, but I caught a ride with my parents, so . . ."

Vi's face fell. "I can give you a ride to the restaurant, but I have to rush off afterward."

"I'll give you a ride home." Spencer's voice was low but definitely directed at her.

Sophie's gaze darted to Emma, whose jaw had hardened. "Oh, you don't have to—"

"That settles it then." Vi tightened her grip on Sophie's arm and steered her toward the lobby. "You're coming with us."

Sophie opened her mouth to protest, but the pleading look in Vi's eyes stopped her. After five years of not being there for her friend, she owed her at least a lunch. "Where to?"

# Chapter 9

"Don't even say it." Spencer held up a hand as he jumped out of his truck and met Emma and the others outside the Hidden Cafe to wait for Violet and Sophie.

"Say what?" Emma's voice was all innocence, but Spencer knew her better than that.

"You were about to lecture me about not falling for Sophie again. But trust me. I've got that covered."

"Yeah, volunteering to drive her home is a good way to keep yourself from getting too close again. I hope you realize I'll be coming with you." She knotted her blond hair—so similar to Sophie's—into a bun at the nape of her neck.

Spencer rolled his eyes. "That won't be necessary."

He'd only known Emma a few years, but sometimes she acted more like a mother than a friend. Then again, he'd been a mess when they'd met, and she'd been the only one he could confide in about how broken Sophie's rejection had left him. The one who had helped him pick up the pieces and move on with his life. He was grateful that she didn't want him to go through that again.

But he didn't need her protection. "For your information, I offered to drive her for Violet's sake." It wasn't entirely a lie. He knew how much seeing Sophie again meant to Violet. Emma didn't need to know how much it meant to him, too.

He smoothed a hand over his hair as Violet's car pulled into the parking lot, Sophie gazing out the passenger window.

Emma snorted. "Look at you, preening for her."

"I'm not preening." But he dropped his hand to his side.

Emma gestured to Ethan and Ariana, who'd been watching them with matching amused grins. "Do you see this?"

Ethan gave Spencer a helpless shrug, and Ariana sent him a sympathetic look.

"I think it's sweet." Ariana smoothed Ethan's hair. "Some people could take a lesson from you."

"You know you like my hair messy." Ethan grinned at her and re-mussed his hair.

Emma huffed out a breath. "You two lovebirds are no help. It's not sweet. We're talking about the woman who ripped his heart out of his chest, ran it through a wood chipper, and then left him to pick up the pieces and stuff them back in."

"Hey." Spencer held up a hand to stop her, but she wasn't far from the truth. In fact, he may have once used those words to describe how he felt when Sophie walked away.

"And—" Emma pointed a finger at his chest. "Don't think I didn't notice the way you two were mooning over each other in church."

Spencer scoffed. "Now I know you're crazy." He'd used every ounce of his willpower to avoid looking at Sophie during church. And when he'd failed and sneaked a glance, her eyes were nowhere near him.

"I'm serious, Spencer." Emma's brow puckered, and she rested a hand on his arm. "You need to be careful."

He relented at Emma's worry.

Maybe she was right.

Maybe he was being too unguarded with his heart.

Sophie opened her car door, and his pulse kicked into overdrive. Apparently, he was about to find out.

⌁

Sophie couldn't believe she'd made it through the meal. Thankfully, Vi had kept her occupied, asking about her life in Chicago and telling her about the antique store. Talking about everything except Spencer and his new girlfriend.

Whose chair was practically on top of Spencer's. And who kept finding excuses to touch him.

Sophie got the message already.

Spencer was taken.

It'd be nice if Emma didn't feel the need to rub it in her face every second.

But that wasn't fair. Of course Emma wanted to touch him. She was in love with him. And she had every right to be.

Sophie had given up her claim to Spencer years ago.

And it had been the right decision.

She knew it had.

She had no doubts.

Or at least none she was willing to examine closely.

She had never wanted to get married and have children. Never fantasized about walking down the aisle or cuddling a baby. It just wasn't her.

The stab she felt every time Emma covered Spencer's hand with her own was only because the last few days had been so difficult.

Nothing else.

She tore her eyes off the spot where Emma's shoulder pressed against Spencer's and focused her attention on Vi. "So, who helps you with the store now—" She broke off abruptly. How could she ever get used to saying that Cade was dead?

"It's just me now." Vi wiped her mouth and pushed her chair back. Apparently not a topic she wanted to talk about.

Sophie and the others pushed their chairs back as well. Sophie swept the check off the table. "This one's on me." The others sent up a stream of protests, and Spencer shot her a hard look. He'd always accused her of trying to buy people's approval.

But that wasn't what this was about. And, anyway, he didn't have a say in what she did anymore.

The others filed out the door as she approached the counter to pay. She appreciated the moment to herself.

But the cashier was too efficient, and after a minute she was outside with everyone else.

She said her goodbyes to the others, promising to see them again before she returned to Chicago. Before she was ready, Vi, Ariana, and Ethan were gone, and she was left standing with Spencer and Emma. She looked back and forth between them, unsure if it would be more awkward if Emma did or didn't come with them.

"I'll see you later," Spencer told Emma.

She pursed her lips but nodded. "Call me." She lifted onto her toes to kiss his cheek.

Sophie looked away.

"Ready?" Spencer's voice sounded strained.

She bobbed her head and followed him. If her parents didn't live five miles out of town and she weren't wearing heels, she'd walk. Actually, walking might be preferable anyway.

But she let Spencer lead her to his black truck. He opened the door for her and held out a hand to help her up.

She wasn't prepared for the jolt that surged up her arm as his hand closed around hers.

She trained her focus on getting into the vehicle, looking at anything but him.

Spencer closed her door, and she tried to slow her revving heart as she fastened her seat belt. Her thoughts skipped over all the things she could say when he got in, but nothing seemed right.

Spencer opened his door and hopped onto his seat in one easy movement.

"Emma seems nice," Sophie blurted. She clamped her mouth shut the moment the words were out. Did she really want to go there?

"Yeah. She is." Spencer's smile crinkled his eyes. Was that the same smile he used to wear when he talked about her?

She swallowed and forced herself to go on. "How long have you two known each other?"

Spencer frowned in thought. "Four years? Maybe five? She bought the horse farm down the road from Hidden Blossom shortly after I moved back. I thought she was crazy at the time. That place was falling apart. But she's really made something of it."

Sophie turned toward the window. A smear of trees blurred past. Emma was a farmer. A much better fit for him than a Chicago developer.

"How's your grandma doing?" Spencer's question brought her back to what really mattered. She shouldn't be worrying about her own lonely life when Nana was dying.

A heavy sigh escaped her. "Not well. She's only been awake for a few minutes at a time. Same old Nana when she is though." She gave a short laugh. "Even managed to talk me into going to church."

Spencer's gaze cut to her. "I'm glad you came."

Sophie shrugged. "I'm not sure it did any good. I haven't been to church in—" But she couldn't even remember the last time. "Years. God has no reason to listen to me."

She ran a knuckle across the cool window, trying not to notice Spencer studying her.

"You know it doesn't work that way, Soph. You don't have to do something for God so he'll listen to you. He loves you."

She shrugged again. If he wanted to believe that, that was fine. But in her experience, nothing ever came without conditions.

Not happiness. Not forgiveness. And definitely not love.

Outside, the trees along the road grew denser as they reached her parents' driveway. Only a few more yards and she'd be free to make her escape.

"How's your dad?"

His forehead creased, the way it always had when he was worried. "He's doing better. But it's hard to see him like this." His jaw jumped. "He's been larger than life to me forever. And now . . ."

He seemed lost in thought, and Sophie waited quietly in case he wanted to continue.

Spencer cleared his throat. "He says thanks for the flowers, by the way."

Sophie's hands stilled. "It's no big deal. I was cutting some for Nana anyway, and I just thought—" What had she thought? It had been a stupid, impetuous move. One Spencer's girlfriend probably didn't appreciate.

"It was a big deal, Soph. Why didn't you tell me you'd been to see him?" Spencer's voice held a thread of gratitude and something else she couldn't place.

She shrugged. It'd been on the tip of her tongue a few times the other night, but she hadn't wanted to overstep her bounds.

"Anyway, he hasn't stopped talking about it." Spencer's lips lifted, and she let herself smile back.

"It was nice to meet him. He reminded me of you."

Spencer's eyes darted to her and then away, and a hint of pink tinged his cheeks. "Well, it meant a lot to him." He cleared his throat again. "And to—"

But he broke off as they rounded the last curve of the driveway. She followed his gaze to the black BMW parked near the house, a man in a sharp suit leaning against the trunk, facing the lake.

Sophie's stomach dropped. She knew only one person who dressed like that on weekends.

"You know him?" Spencer's voice had taken on a funny, raspy quality.

Sophie nodded dumbly, trying to process. "He's my . . ." But her brain had closed up shop. What did she call Chase? And what was he doing here?

"Ah." The single syllable said everything Spencer was thinking. She opened her mouth to correct him, but what difference did it make? He was with Emma anyway, so he couldn't care less if she was with someone else.

"Thanks for the ride." She fumbled for the door handle, her eyes fixed on Chase, who marched toward the truck with his long, confident strides and Armani suit that was so out of place here.

"You're welcome." Spencer hit the unlock button, and she shoved out the door and slammed it behind her before Chase reached them. There was no need for these two to meet.

The moment she took a step away from the truck, the tires crunched over the blacktop.

"Surprise!" Chase dropped a quick kiss on her lips. She took a step back and glanced over her shoulder, but Spencer's truck was already retreating down the driveway.

She tried to infuse something close to enthusiasm into her voice. "Chase! What are you doing here?"

# Chapter 10

Spencer's knuckles stood out white against the steering wheel.

He had only himself to blame for letting his heart go where it wasn't supposed to go. Served him right for offering to drive Sophie home. For admiring the way her hair fell in a curtain around her face when she ducked her head in embarrassment. For basking in every little smile she sent his way. For thinking that she'd felt the same familiar spark he had the other night.

He unclenched one fist, lifted it from the wheel, then slammed it back into place. Emma had been right. When it came to Sophie, he had no common sense.

Case in point: He'd forbidden himself from looking in the rearview mirror as he'd left Sophie's parents' house. But his resolve had lasted all of three seconds. He'd glanced into the mirror just in time to see that man—that good-looking, well-dressed, BMW-driving man—kiss her.

Spencer stretched his ear toward his shoulder, trying to release the tension that had seized his neck.

He had to face it. The man Sophie was with now—that was the kind of man she deserved to be with. Someone who could give her the kind of life she'd always had. The kind of life she'd always wanted. The kind of life he could never offer.

Sure, he'd been good enough for a college boyfriend. Good enough for someone to hang out with. But when she'd had to consider the kind of man she wanted to spend the rest of her life with, he hadn't measured up.

Spencer shook himself. He'd already gotten over Sophie. There was no reason to get so worked up over the fact that she'd found someone else. It's not like he hadn't imagined a thousand times the kind of man she'd end up with. A man just like the one with her right now.

He pulled into Hidden Blossom's driveway, slowing to examine the rambling farmhouse he'd grown up in. The paint had been peeling since before he was born. But now it was in desperate need of repainting. Shingles were peeling up in several places as well. But with Dad's new medical expenses, both things would have to wait.

Spencer was plenty used to doing without, but it hurt to see his parents still struggling after all these years. It seemed life on the farm never got easier.

Another reason it was best he stopped dreaming about Sophie. He had to give all his attention to helping his family.

Speaking of—

Spencer leaned forward as he approached his house. An unfamiliar car was parked in front of the shed. His eyes traveled past the car to his front lawn.

The old farm dog Buck must have followed the car to the house and was now trying to sniff two small boys, who kept running away. Their shrieks cut through Spencer's window, and he grinned as he caught sight of his brother chasing the boys. Every time Tyler caught one of them, the other ran off, screaming even louder. Buck chased along, apparently finding the whole thing one big game.

Spencer was tempted to stop the truck right here so he could just sit watching his brother and nephews. The weight that had been pressing on him lightened. He hadn't realized how much he missed his brother until this moment, seeing him again. And the boys reminded him of himself and Tyler when they were younger.

He pulled into the driveway next to Tyler's car. The moment his big brother's eyes fell on him, relief took over his face.

Spencer shoved his door open and jumped from the truck, calling the dog to him.

He ordered Buck to heel and led him slowly into the yard. He told the dog to sit. Buck obeyed, his tongue lolling to the side, and gave Spencer a pleading look as if to ask, "Can we play again?"

"Stay," Spencer commanded. Then he crouched at Buck's side. He patted the dog's head with one hand and held out his other hand to the boy latched to Tyler's leg. "See, he's a nice doggy." As if to prove the point, Buck swiped his tongue down Spencer's cheek.

The little boy laughed and took a small step closer.

"This is Buck. You can pet him," Spencer said. "Maybe he'll give you a kiss, too."

The boy giggled again and toddled closer. His brother watched from Tyler's arms, letting out an occasional cry.

As soon as the closer twin was within reach, Buck stuck his snout forward to sniff. The boy let out another scream and almost toppled over backward, but Spencer grabbed his hand. It was sticky and a little wet but warm, and it made something pull in Spencer's gut. This was his nephew.

"It's okay," he soothed. "The doggy just wants to sniff you. That's how doggies say hi."

The boy looked from Spencer to the dog, then took a tiny step forward. This time when Buck sniffed him, he giggled. "It tickles."

Spencer laughed and the boy stepped right up to Buck, petting the dog's ear. Buck used the opportunity to lick the boy's nose. The twin giggled harder, and from behind him, his brother joined in.

Soon, both boys were petting the dog and taking turns getting dog kisses.

Spencer pushed to his feet and met his brother's eyes. Tyler held out a tentative hand, but Spencer pulled him in for a quick hug. "It's good to see you, man. I'm glad you came."

Tyler slapped Spencer's back. "Thank goodness you showed up when you did. I was about ready to throw the boys back in the car and take off. And I'm not sure I could have handled another ten-hour drive with these two. Julia always—" His voice cracked, and he scanned the farm, face gathered into a frown. "Gotta say, I never thought I'd be back here again."

Spencer clapped his brother's shoulder. "Ah, it's not so bad here. You might even find you like it."

At his feet, the twins were fighting over who got the next "Bucky kiss." Spencer bent to scoop one twin up in each of his arms, relishing their heft. "Enough love for the dog. What about your uncle Spencer? He's way cooler than a dog. And he can give kisses, too." He flicked his tongue at the twins, who squealed and tried to squirm away.

But Spencer pulled them closer, and they wrapped their little arms around his neck, letting him carry them inside.

Sophie massaged her temples, trying to ease the splitting headache that had kicked in right around the time she found Chase outside her parents' house. Apparently, he'd already arranged everything with her mother and would be spending the night here. The second guest room was being prepared for him.

"You really didn't have to come," she said for at least the eighth time as she sat stiffly on the straight-backed chair in the formal living room.

"I told you, I missed you." Chase leaned forward and reached to squeeze her hand. She tried to squeeze back, quashing down the guilt at the fact that she had barely thought of him since she'd left Chicago.

"So what's there to do around here?" Chase's eyes fell on the picture windows overlooking the lake. "You must have a boat, right? Should we take her out for a ride?"

Sophie frowned at him. It was already way past the time she should be at Nana's. "I was planning to spend the day at the hospital." She gestured toward the window. "But you're welcome to check out the lake. There's a great public pier next to the marina downtown."

Chase sighed, not bothering to hide his pout. "No, that's okay. I'll go with you."

*Don't do me any favors.*

But Sophie gave him a tight smile. "That sounds nice."

She led the way to the front closet and grabbed a light jacket. Chase plucked it from her grip and held it up to help her into it. Sophie gritted her teeth, then forced herself to relax.

Why was she so annoyed with everything he did right now? He was only trying to be thoughtful. He'd driven all the way from Chicago, after all. He wouldn't have had to do that.

She tried to ignore the fact that he hadn't asked about her grandmother. Hadn't apologized for dropping in on her unexpectedly. Hadn't really seemed to think of her at all.

Still, she resolved to give Chase the benefit of the doubt.

She opened the front door but stopped short at the sight of Mom standing on the top step, staring out toward the lake. "Mom?"

Mom jumped and spun toward her. "Oh, Sophie, you startled me." Her eyes fell on Chase, and her smile warmed. "I hope you have everything you need."

Chase gave her the suave smile that had helped him close plenty of deals. "And then some."

"Good." Mom stepped to the door as Sophie and Chase started down the steps. "Where are you kids off to?"

"To visit Nana."

"Sophie." Her mother's tone held the familiar reprimand. "You two should go and do something fun. Nana won't mind."

Sophie bit her tongue to keep from asking how Mom would know what Nana would or wouldn't mind, when she hadn't been to visit her once since she'd been in the hospital.

"I promised Nana," she said simply.

"Well at least go out to dinner afterward." Mom stepped into the house. "Take him to Alessandro's." She turned to Chase. "It's divine."

Sophie puffed out an irritated breath as Mom closed the door. "Sorry about her."

But Chase had pulled out his phone and was lifting it to his ear.

"What are you doing?"

Chase waved a hand to shush her. "Making reservations." He gave his attention to someone on the other end of the phone.

Sophie rolled her eyes and led the way to her car. It was going to be a long afternoon.

Chase got off the phone as Sophie directed the car toward town. For the next ten minutes, he filled her in on the latest details on the Hudson project. She tried to bring her thoughts into focus on what he was saying. It would give her a leg up when she got back to the office.

But her mind refused to cooperate. It kept rewinding to earlier that afternoon. To the way Spencer had thanked her for visiting his dad. To the way he'd tensed when he saw Chase.

She signaled and turned onto Hope Street. Early-season tourists were out in full force today, and Sophie craned her neck to spot Vi's antique shop.

There.

Tucked right next to the fudge shop.

"Well, this is quaint." Chase didn't bother to mask his derision. Clearly, to him quaint meant backward.

Sophie tightened her hands on the wheel but then forced them to relax. After all, she'd thought of her hometown that way more than once. Since she'd been back, though, quaint had started to seem like a good thing.

She shook herself. Quaint might be fine for a visit. But her life was in the city.

With Chase.

Not here. Not with Spencer, who even now refused to exit her thoughts.

That had to stop.

She pulled into the hospital parking lot and turned to Chase. "Thanks for—"

But his phone rang, and he shifted his attention to the screen.

"Sorry, I have to take this." Chase answered the call before she could respond.

She sighed and stepped out of the car, waiting for Chase to join her. Even though he was on the phone and had no idea where they were going, he took the lead. She sped up to match his long strides, occasionally pointing to keep him going in the right direction.

By the time they reached Nana's room, he still wasn't off the phone. Sophie waited a few minutes, but when he didn't show any sign of wrapping up the call, she entered the room alone.

"Hi, Nana." She'd finally gotten used to talking to her grandmother when she was sleeping. Nana's form seemed to have shrunk since yesterday so that she looked almost like the toothpick figure Sophie had once constructed for a school project.

Sophie crossed the room to open the curtains. Streamers of white-gold light speckled the floor. "It's nice out today. The lake was so glassy this morning. Made me think of that time we went over to Strawberry Island. Remember? The water was so flat you said we should try walking on it." She paused, gazing out the window. "So I tried. But I couldn't, obviously. And then you held me up, so I'd feel like I really was walking on the water. And you told me—" Sophie swallowed and crossed the room to Nana's bedside. She brushed at the wispy strands of hair that poked up from Nana's head. "You told me that you'd always try to hold me up, but when you couldn't God would still be there, holding me." She settled into the chair next to Nana's bed and blew out a slow breath. A shadow of the truth had been nagging at her for the past couple days, and being in church this morning had only given it substance. "But, Nana." Her voice came out as little more than a whisper. "I've pushed God away. I'm not sure he's holding me anymore."

She tried to shove down the confusion that had overcome her this week. She wasn't used to being so unsure. She willed Nana to wake up. To tell her how to fix this. But Nana didn't stir.

"Glad that's taken care of." Chase's over-loud voice ricocheted around the room. Sophie cringed and held a finger to her lips.

"Oh, sorry." Chase lowered his voice. His face had paled, and his eyes darted around the room, as if searching for a safe place to land.

"Here." Sophie moved to bring the other chair in the room closer, but Chase shook his head.

"I'm good." He anchored himself on the narrow windowsill.

"Okay then." Sophie's eyes flicked from Chase to Nana. "Nana, this is Chase. He's my—" She fumbled. "We work together. Chase, this is my grandmother."

Chase gave a quick nod but didn't look at Nana.

"It's okay." Sophie hadn't pegged him for squeamish. "You can talk to her."

Chase gave her a blank stare. "She's out."

"I know." Sophie moved back to her chair. "You get used to it."

Chase nodded again but didn't say anything.

Sophie chewed her lip. Having him here made her self-conscious about talking to Nana, too.

So she just sat, holding Nana's hand.

Out of the corner of her eye, she saw Chase pull out his phone. After a quick glance, he heaved a noticeable sigh and clicked it off.

Five minutes later, he did the same thing.

And five minutes after that.

Finally, Sophie couldn't take it anymore. "Why don't you go check out the pier? It's a few blocks to the north. I'll meet you there in a bit."

The relief that passed over Chase's face was almost comical. "You sure?"

But he was already striding toward the door.

She tensed as he detoured to drop a kiss onto her cheek.

The door clicked, and an overwhelming peace settled over the room.

Sophie squeezed Nana's hand. "Now, where were we?"

# Chapter 11

Spencer wanted to yank the hair out of his head.

He had been listening to two screaming boys for an hour and a half, and he was pretty sure he was going to lose his mind if it didn't stop soon.

"Let's try the bears again," he yelled to his brother over the screams.

Tyler nodded, his jaw tense, as he pulled Jonah to him.

Spencer grabbed Jeremiah and tried to give him the stuffed bear he'd dug out of an old box in his parents' attic. But the toddler chucked it into the wall on the other side of the room. Kid had a surprisingly good arm. Maybe he'd play football someday.

If they all survived this night.

On the other side of the room, Tyler was having no better luck. Little Jonah was stomping on his bear's head.

"I give up." Tyler set Jonah down and dropped into the unpainted rocking chair Spencer had brought in from the shed.

He buried his face in his hands. "They want their mommy." His voice was muffled through his fingers, but Spencer heard the pain in it. "I want her, too."

Spencer retrieved the two bears and set them on the dresser.

He glanced at the window. It was so dark outside. Maybe the boys needed a night-light.

Not that he had any of those lying around. But maybe—

"Hold on." He jogged out of the room as the twins resumed their screaming behind him.

He pushed out the front door and jogged down the porch steps and across the yard to the workshop.

He'd brought a small reading lamp out here a few weeks ago to help him see the fine details better in the dark space.

As he crossed the workshop, his eyes fell on the bench he'd made for Sophie months before proposing to her. It was supposed to be a wedding present.

How had he been so sure she'd say yes? How had he been so wrong about their relationship?

And now, all these years later, he still couldn't bring himself to get rid of it. Maybe he should sell it. Make a few bucks off it, at least.

But getting rid of it felt too permanent. Like he was giving up all hope of ever being with Sophie.

*Not that there's anything to hope for anyway. You saw her kissing another man. What more proof that she's over you do you need? An invitation to their wedding?*

Spencer yanked the lamp off his workbench with a snarl at himself. He was being stupid, thinking about Sophie, when he had two screaming nephews and a heartbroken brother to take care of.

He grabbed the lamp and sprinted to the house without another glance at the bench.

If possible, the volume of the wailing had increased. Both boys were in the portable cribs Tyler had brought along, standing with their hands gripping the sides. Streaks of tears and dirt clung to their splotchy cheeks, and snot dripped toward their mouths. If he hadn't seen much worse helping Emma deliver horses, Spencer would be disgusted.

Tyler stood between the two cribs, shoulders hunched, arms hanging limply at his sides.

"Here we go." Spencer tried the soothing voice he used with Emma's horses whenever they were spooked. He clicked on the reading lamp, then turned off the overhead light.

The boys went silent for a moment, and Spencer held his breath. Had he really solved the problem?

He was a hero.

Super Uncle.

Spencer the Great.

He was—

The wailing started again.

Spencer groaned.

Tyler spun his back to them, fists on his forehead. "How am I ever going to do this?"

Spencer crossed to his brother and wrapped an arm around his shoulder, leading him toward the door. "Go. Take a walk or something. I'll handle this."

Tyler shook his head. "You'll handle it?"

*I always do.* But Spencer bit back the words. Now was not the time.

Tyler opened his mouth again, then nodded once and left the room. A second later, the front door banged shut.

"There, now it's just you and me, boys." Spencer moved into the rocking chair. "Tell you what. I'm going to sit here and listen to you two scream. And when you tire yourselves out with that, you can lay down and go to sleep, okay?"

But the twins had more willpower than Spencer had given them credit for. After twenty minutes, he considered joining in the screaming. Anything would be better than listening to it.

He needed backup.

But his mom had been staying at the hospital with his dad, and he didn't want to wake her in case she was actually managing to get some sleep.

He'd always assumed that when he got to the point of dealing with screaming children, it'd be with Sophie at his side as they made their own family memories. But if she was going to be taking care of kids with anyone, it was with Mr. BMW.

What about Emma? She took care of baby horses all the time. Maybe she'd know what to do with baby humans, too.

He sent her a quick, desperate text.

A few seconds later, she texted him back. *Try this. Helps me sleep.*

There was a link attached. Spencer clicked it, and it took him to a video. Relaxing Horse Galloping Sound Effects.

Spencer stared at it, then shrugged and hit play. He was willing to try anything at this point.

It took the boys a few seconds to notice the sounds of horse hooves and waves, but as they did, they quieted to listen.

Spencer turned up the volume on his phone a notch.

The boys yawned and rubbed their eyes.

Ten minutes later, both laid down.

Spencer closed his own eyes, letting the sound of their soft breathing mingle with the horse hoofbeats.

Maybe this was what peace felt like.

"Finally," Chase breathed into Sophie's ear as they entered Alessandro's. "Somewhere civilized."

Sophie's hands clenched. *Only a few more hours.*

Then she could go to bed. And escape Chase. At least until morning.

She caught herself before she groaned out loud.

Whatever it was about him that had appealed to her in Chicago had lost its luster in her hometown. There, he seemed confident and in control. Here, it was more like pompous and overbearing.

Earlier, when she'd rejoined him at the pier after her visit with Nana, he'd lunged at her in relief, as if she'd abandoned him in the wild for days.

"Glad that's over with." He'd given her his deprecating smile. "You would not believe how many little brats have taken over this pier in the past hour."

Sophie hadn't bothered to point out that it had only been half an hour. That she'd cut her time with Nana short because she'd known he'd be getting impatient.

It had been too early for their reservation, though, so she'd driven him to see the sights the peninsula was known for—the farmer's market, the giant sunfish statue, the Old Lighthouse. His reaction to each had been the same: indifference.

Finally, she'd given up and they'd come to Alessandro's early. At least Chase would be content waiting here. In his element.

The maître d' took their name and ushered them to an elegant lounge with high chandeliers and plush carpeting to wait.

"I'll get us some drinks." Chase disappeared without asking what she'd like.

Sophie scrutinized the space as she sank into a supple leather chair. Her parents had brought her here for countless birthdays, even when all she'd wanted was a simple party at home. She'd always felt like she was on display here, her parents showing her off to all their country club friends. And those friends boasting of their own children's achievements, which always outshone hers, until, by the end of the night, she could feel her parents' disappointment radiating off them.

Her eyes fell on Evelyn and Andrew Carter, and she sent up a small plea. Maybe they wouldn't notice her.

But as if drawn by the thought, Evelyn's eyes landed right on her. The woman's diamond tennis bracelet sparked in the light as she tapped her husband's shoulder and pointed at Sophie, then gave an exaggerated wave.

Sophie gritted her teeth but raised her hand in a small wave. The Carters were already on their way toward her.

Sophie pushed her lips into a painful smile as they reached her. "Mr. And Mrs. Carter. It's so nice to see you."

"And you, dear." Mrs. Carter leaned in to give Sophie a kiss on each cheek. "How are your parents?"

"They're fine." Sophie kept her answer short. Maybe once the pleasantries were over, the Carters would move on.

"And what brings you back to Hope Springs, dear? Our Myla is so busy she never makes it home. She's a resident now, you know. Neurosurgery."

Sophie grimaced. She had no interest in knowing what her oldest rival was up to—though the two girls probably never would have become rivals if their parents hadn't constantly pitted them against each other.

"My grandma is ill." Sophie kept her tone civil but hoped the Carters would get the hint that she was done talking.

"Oh, I did hear that. Myla's grandmother died last year, but she was so busy she couldn't make it back. We all understood, though. You're lucky your job is so much less demanding." Evelyn's eyes traveled down Sophie's simple black dress. "What is it you do now, dear?" If the woman were any more patronizing, she'd pat Sophie on the head and hand her a lollipop.

Before Sophie could answer, she spotted Chase. She'd never been so grateful to see him. "I'll let you go. I should get back to my—" She gestured toward Chase.

"Oh, yes, I see." Evelyn's sharp laugh punched through the air and Sophie winced. "Poor Myla hasn't found herself a man yet. But she has time, of course. I'm always telling her to get her career off the ground first and then—" She broke off as Chase reached them.

He passed Sophie a glass of wine and held out a hand to Evelyn. "I don't believe we've met. I'm Chase."

Evelyn's eyes flicked to Chase's tailored suit and handmade patent leather shoes. She looked mildly impressed. "Evelyn Carter. The Olsens are good friends of ours. Aren't they dear?" She gestured to her husband, who had yet to say a word.

The hostess approached the group. "Table for two for Sanders."

"That's us." Sophie barely masked her relief.

"Well, it was lovely seeing you, dear." Evelyn held out a hand to Chase again. "And delightful to meet you. I'm sure we'll be seeing plenty more of you. Be sure to invite us to the wedding."

That was enough of that. Sophie practically shoved Chase toward the hostess.

"Evelyn seemed nice," Chase said once they were seated. "Your family is close to theirs?"

Sophie shook her head. She didn't really want to talk about the Carters. But she couldn't think of anything else to talk about. "They've been friends with my parents since before I was born. They have a daughter my age. Myla." Even the name left a bad taste in her mouth.

Chase snickered. "What's so bad about Myla?"

Sophie wrinkled her nose. "Nothing."

"Come on." Chase nudged her leg with his under the table. "Let me dislike her with you."

Sophie couldn't help but laugh. "Well, she was always super-competitive, for one. Constantly trying to one-up me. And her parents encouraged it." As did Sophie's. She could still picture her parents' expressions when they'd learned she'd be graduating second in her class, behind Myla. "And she couldn't let an argument go. Always had to have the last word. And—"

But, no. She was a bigger person than this. She was successful now. She didn't have to compare herself to Myla or anyone else.

Chase raised an eyebrow at her, waiting.

Fine.

"And she was so— So driven. Nothing mattered to her but being the best." And making Sophie feel the sting of her own inferiority.

Chase's eyebrow remained hiked. "So she was basically you?"

Sophie opened her mouth to argue. She was nothing like Myla.

Except maybe she was.

The thought slammed back and forth in her head. Was that really who she was? Someone who thought only about her own achievements, about the next thing she needed to do to get ahead?

Her jaw snapped shut.

"So, anyway, the Hudson project . . ." Chase picked up the subject as if he hadn't just blindsided her with his comment.

She grabbed her wine glass with shaky hands. Was Chase the only one who saw her this way, or did everyone?

Did Spencer?

But she already knew the answer. She swallowed the bitter drink and pretended to listen to Chase for the rest of the meal, interjecting the occasional "yes" or "uh-huh." If Chase noticed she wasn't giving him her full attention—or even a tenth of it—he didn't seem to mind.

"Now what?" Chase asked as he finally pushed his plate to the side.

Sophie lifted a last bite of duck confit to her mouth. Even as the rich flavor coated her tongue, all she could think about was how much she could go for a pizza.

"We could take a walk." Fresh air would do her good. "The beach is always pretty at night. There are these amazing sand dunes."

Chase frowned. "In these shoes? And you're wearing your favorite Manolo Blahniks."

She shrugged. "We could take them off. Go barefoot." It seemed to be a thing with her lately anyway.

He wrinkled his nose. "I was thinking a little more upscale. Any clubs around here?"

Sophie laughed. "Not exactly. This town pretty much shuts down by ten. Actually, I kind of have a headache. Do you mind if we go back to my parents' place?"

Chase gave a heavy sigh. "Yeah, okay."

She was unmoved by his pouty act.

The drive to her parents' house was blissfully silent, and Sophie spent the time dreaming of snuggling into her favorite pajamas and curling up with a book before going to sleep.

When they reached the house, Sophie led the way upstairs to the guest bedrooms. She paused at her bedroom door. "Goodnight, Chase. Thanks for dinner."

Instead of passing her to move to his own room, he stopped, too. His eyes traveled to the spot where her dress strap slipped from her shoulder.

Before she realized what he was doing, he'd moved in and pressed his lips to hers, his hands coming to her arms.

Sophie stiffened and pulled her head back, shoving a hand against his chest.

"What's wrong?" He grabbed her hand and tugged her closer.

"Chase—"

He didn't let go of her, but he did stop trying to pull her to him. "What is it?"

She couldn't tell if it was hurt in his expression or petulance.

She didn't want to make things awkward. But she had to be honest. "I don't think our relationship is a good idea."

He held up a hand. "You're worried about your job. I get it. But I've already spoken to my father about this. It's not like I'm going to pursue a relationship that could destroy my career."

*How sweet.*

But he was still talking. "I explained to my father that our relationship is like a business partnership with benefits." He brought his mouth closer to hers. "Like this."

She swiveled her head so that his lips landed on her cheek.

She reached behind her and fumbled for the doorknob. "It's not going to work, Chase."

"But Sophie—" His voice grew hard. He was used to getting his way.

"I'm sorry, Chase." Her hand connected with the knob, and she shoved the door open. "I think you should go home in the morning."

Chase's face reddened. But Sophie stepped into her room and pushed the door closed behind her.

A few seconds later, she heard the door to Chase's room next door close hard.

She crossed the room and laid on her bed, fully clothed.

A business partnership? Is that really the kind of relationship Chase thought she wanted?

Then again, why wouldn't he think that? Almost the only thing the two of them had in common was work. And most of their dates centered on talk of the latest projects. What else would he think?

She stared at the ceiling, wrapping her arms around her middle. Something big and empty had opened inside her. Even though she could hear Chase in the next room, all she could see was Spencer.

The relationship he'd offered her once hadn't been a business partnership. It'd been one based on joy in being together. On a commitment to the same values. On love.

She squeezed her arms tighter.

She'd been so sure then that she didn't want what he was offering. Didn't want love and family.

But it turned out he'd been offering her everything she needed.

And she hadn't realized it until this moment.

When it was too late.

# Chapter 12

Sophie stabbed at a piece of cantaloupe and brought it to her mouth mechanically. Chase had left before she'd gotten up this morning, without so much as a goodbye. Which meant things would be worse than awkward when she got back to Chicago. But that was a problem for another day. What was it Nana had always said? "Each day has enough trouble of its own." That was from the Bible, if Sophie remembered her Sunday school lessons correctly.

A sharp click of heels on the floor announced Mom's arrival. Sophie tensed and sat up straighter. She'd promised herself she'd have this conversation with Mom, but she wasn't eager to do it.

"Morning." Mom went straight for the coffee.

Sophie took a deep breath, but Mom spoke first. "Where's your boyfriend?"

Sophie blinked. "Boyfriend? Oh, Chase? We weren't really— I mean, we went on a few dates, but—" Why did it matter to her what Mom thought about this? "Anyway, he left early this morning."

Her mother frowned. "So soon? He just got here."

"Yeah, well, I asked him to leave."

Mom lowered her coffee cup. "Why would you do that?"

Sophie shrugged. She and Mom had never talked about this kind of stuff. Nana had always been the one Sophie confided in. "We aren't right for each other."

Mom snorted. "Yeah, successful businessmen who also happen to be the son of the owner always make the worst matches."

Sophie gawked at her mother. Did she really expect Sophie to be in a relationship to further her career?

"I'm going to visit Nana. I think you should come with me."

Mom drained her coffee cup and turned to the sink to rinse it. Then she grabbed the rag and wiped at the already-clean counter.

Sophie opened her mouth to repeat her request even though she knew Mom had heard her the first time.

But Mom beat her to it. "I'm not going."

Exactly what Sophie had expected. But she was ready for it. "I know it's hard for you, after Jordan." Her mother's shoulders hardened, but Sophie pressed on. "It's hard for me, too."

"I'm not going—" Mom's voice was too calm, too quiet.

"But, Nana—"

"I said no."

Sophie bit her lip. If it were about anything else, she'd retreat. But she couldn't this time. It was too important. If Mom didn't say goodbye to Nana, she'd be left with regrets the rest of her life.

"You know what I think, Mom?" Sophie moved closer and laid a hand tentatively on Mom's arm.

Mom looked from Sophie's face to the spot where Sophie's hand rested on her arm. Then she very deliberately took a step away.

She spun on her heel and strode from the room.

Sophie sighed.

She'd longed so many times for a relationship with her mother.

But it looked like that was just one more thing she couldn't have.

&#8767;

Spencer's arms throbbed with the weight of his nephew, but he wasn't about to put the boy down. He'd been dragging his brother and the twins around town to show them the sights all morning. It was a good way to distract them from missing Julia. And to show them off, if he was honest.

They'd already visited the pier, the toy store, and the fudge shop, where Ariana cooed over the boys and plied them with too much fudge.

Jonah rubbed his chocolate-streaked face against Spencer's shirt.

"Hey." Spencer tickled the boy, eliciting a contagious giggle.

"You up for one more stop?" Spencer asked his brother.

"Lead the way." Tyler's eyes had grown brighter throughout the morning, his gait more sure.

"Good. Violet would never forgive me if I didn't bring these two to meet her." He stopped outside the antique shop.

Tyler's forehead crinkled. "You want to bring them into a store full of breakables?"

Spencer eyed the store, then his nephews, whose eyelids were starting to droop after the long morning. "They'll be fine."

Tyler shook his head as Spencer pulled the door open and gestured for him to enter. "I hope you have your credit card ready."

"Relax. It'll be—"

But the moment he followed his brother into the shop, he rethought his assessment.

Not because of the breakables.

But because of the person standing at the counter talking to Violet.

Sophie.

His eyes flicked around the store. If Sophie was here, her boyfriend must be, too. His grip on Jonah tightened. He couldn't deal with this right now. The urge to flee seized him. Was it too late to back quietly through the door?

But Violet had already spotted Tyler and was headed toward them.

"And who are these two?" she asked with a wide smile.

Sophie turned then, too.

She did a double-take as her eyes fell on Spencer. Jonah had lain his head on Spencer's shoulder. The boy's soft breaths puffed onto Spencer's neck. It was oddly reassuring.

"Violet. Sophie. This is my brother Tyler. And these little terrors"—he gestured with his chin toward Jeremiah, whose head dropped against Tyler's chest—"are my nephews Jeremiah and Jonah."

Violet crossed the space to shake Tyler's hand. "Yeah, they look like real terrors, about to fall asleep in your arms."

"That's because they're so exhausted from screaming all night." The hair on the back of Spencer's neck lifted at the thought of going through all that again tonight.

Violet laughed. "It couldn't have been that bad."

Spencer groaned. "Worse. Thank goodness for Emma. She had this horse hoofbeat soundtrack, and it put them right to sleep."

Across the room, Sophie's head jerked up, but she didn't make eye contact.

Violet turned to Tyler. "So how long will you be staying in Hope Springs?"

Tyler's eyes widened, and he looked for all the world like the raccoon Buck had treed last fall. "I'm not sure yet."

"You married Julia, right?" Violet pressed on, apparently oblivious to the fact that her signature hospitality was killing his brother. "How's she doing?"

Tyler opened and closed his mouth. "Uh—"

Spencer jumped in. "Where's your friend?" he shot at Sophie. "How long's he staying?" He shouldn't have said it. He didn't want to know the answer.

"He's not—" Sophie started, but her phone gave a sharp blast that made her jump. The moment she looked at the screen, her brows drew together, and she lifted the phone to her ear.

"This is she," she said after a second.

As she listened to the caller, her face went white and she pressed her lips together, drawing her hand to her forehead as if shielding her eyes from the sunlight.

Spencer was moving before he realized it, passing Jonah to Tyler and crossing the store to stand at Sophie's elbow.

She didn't look at him.

After a moment she spoke into the phone. "Thank you for letting me know. I'll be right there."

She hung up the phone but stood staring at it. Her ragged breaths tugged Spencer closer.

"Sophie?" He reached toward her.

"That was, um—" She licked her lips and swallowed. "That was the hospital. It's my grandma. She's gone."

Spencer didn't think. He just leaned over and wrapped his arms around her, pulling her into him.

She didn't resist. Her arms went around his back, and she buried her face in his neck.

Spencer could feel his heart slipping.

But he didn't care.

Right now it wasn't his own heart he was worried about.

Right now, he would give anything to heal the pain in hers.

<hr />

Sophie clutched Nana's cold hand, swallowing over and over to keep the tears at bay.

Seeing her grandmother like this made her feel like the first time she'd ever been on a boat—wobbly all over, as if the laws of physics no longer applied to standing still.

She swayed, but a firm arm wrapped around her from behind and held her up.

"It's okay." Spencer's voice was low, steady. Reassuring.

Sophie took in a couple of deep breaths, letting his presence calm her.

"She looks so—" Sophie couldn't think of the word to describe how Nana looked.

"Gone, I guess," she finished.

Spencer's hand moved in small circles on her back. He'd sent Tyler and the twins home in his truck and insisted on driving her to the hospital.

A flood of memories threatened to drown her. Nana standing at the helm of her boat, the sun hat she'd perched on her head flying off in the breeze. Or pulling a fresh batch of cookies from the oven, a dusting of flour on her nose. Bandaging yet another scraped knee Sophie had managed to get roller skating because she could never get her gangly legs under control.

Nana was in heaven now, like she'd wanted. She'd been ready.

But Sophie wasn't.

A light tap on the door was followed by soft footsteps. "Doing okay in here?" It was the nurse who had led them into the room half an hour earlier. She'd become Sophie's favorite in the last few days. Always attentive. Always seeming to know when Sophie needed to talk and when she needed to be left alone with her thoughts.

Sophie nodded. She couldn't find her voice.

"Take your time." The nurse laid a small canvas bag on the table near the bed. "Feel free to use this to pack up your grandmother's things. Or we can do that for you if you'd prefer."

Sophie shook her head and shot a desperate look at Spencer.

"We'll do it," he told the nurse.

The nurse patted Sophie's shoulder on her way past. "I'm sorry for your loss. Your grandma was a special lady." She paused in the doorway, as if deliberating. "When she first came in, she talked to me a lot. I'd fallen away in my faith because of—" She waved a hand. "Well, for a lot of reasons. But your grandma helped me see God again." The woman ducked her head.

When she lifted it, her eyes were shining. "She made a big difference in my life."

Sophie pressed her lips together. Why couldn't she have gotten here sooner, so she could have had more of those conversations with Nana? She hadn't even realized she needed to talk about those things until she'd come home. And now that she wanted to talk, she had no one to talk to.

Spencer gave her arm a gentle squeeze. "I'll pack up this stuff."

As he stepped around the bed, she was seized with the urge to grab him and pull him back toward her. Having him here was the only thing getting her through this. But he'd only come because he was a good man. He had a girlfriend, his own life, to get back to.

She moved Nana's arm and settled onto the bed next to her motionless form. "I'll miss you, Nana."

On the other side of the room, Spencer quietly emptied the chest of drawers that held Nana's possessions. Sophie kept talking to Nana. It wasn't weird with Spencer here, the way it had been with Chase.

"Uh, Soph?" Spencer interjected when she fell silent.

She lifted her head. Spencer was standing over the chest of drawers, holding a thick leather journal. "I think you should see this." He crossed the room and held it out to her.

Sophie's hand closed around the leather, and her breath caught. Embossed in gold on the cover were the words "Sophie's Wisdom."

"What is this?" She lifted the cover carefully as if the book were a rare treasure. Inside, the first page was covered with Nana's familiar, small handwriting. Sophie fanned through the rest of the book. Nearly every page was filled. She flipped back to the beginning and read out loud.

"My dearest Sophia. You were born today, and what a precious child you are. I am starting this journal for you to share the things I've learned in my life that you may not be ready to learn for a long time. But when you are, they will be here for you, even if I'm not."

Sophie cut off, swallowing down the sobs that threatened to overtake her. From the day she was born, Nana had been thinking about what she'd need for her future. And what had Sophie done for Nana?

Left her.

Ignored her.

She turned back to the page, but the words blurred.

A gentle hand lifted the book from hers. "Your name means wisdom." Spencer's voice was low and sure as he read. "It's a fitting name. My prayer for you, on the day of your birth, is that you would turn away from the wisdom of this world. From a desire for fame and glory and achievement. For recognition from people. That wisdom is too fleeting, too easily lost. I pray that you seek instead the wisdom from above. The wisdom that tells you that you are loved unconditionally by your heavenly father. And by me."

Spencer stopped reading and wrapped an arm around her shoulders, pulling her in close.

"I don't deserve that," she choked out.

Spencer's laugh was gentle. "That's why they call it unconditional."

Sophie pressed her face into his chest and let him hold her. Just for today, she'd let herself believe that was true. It was better than admitting she hadn't come close to living up to Nana's expectations.

# Chapter 13

Sophie's whole body felt like a spring that had been coiled beyond the breaking point.

She rubbed her heavy eyes, relieved for the break in the receiving line. She knew it was a testament to how many lives Nana had touched that the line had stretched to the back of the church for the past hour, but if she had to accept one more person's condolences, she was going to lose her hold on the emotions that had hovered at the back of her throat for the three days since Nana's death. Three days that she'd spent holed up in her room, reading Nana's journal. Though its words brought her comfort, they also scraped at her already raw heart.

Sophie glanced at her parents, one on each side of her. She longed for them to grab her hands, to squish her between them the way they had after Jordan's death. But neither even seemed to care that she was there.

"I'll be right back." She said the words to both—or neither, she wasn't sure. "I need some water."

In the lobby, Sophie let out a long breath, then forced herself to inhale for a ten-count.

Now that she was out here, she realized she needed fresh air more than water. She pushed through the lobby doors.

Outside, a thick fog had rolled in, cloaking everything in a gray mantle. She caught the scent of the lake.

What if she . . .

Before she could complete the thought, she'd kicked her shoes off and dashed to the steps that ran alongside the church and down to the beach below.

The cool sand curled over her toes.

She dropped her shoes and made her way to the spot where the waves licked the shore.

The sharp cold of the water sent pinpricks up her feet.

"What do you want from me?" The words ripped out of her as she peered into the nothingness of the fog. She didn't know who her question was directed to, only that she was desperate for an answer. "How am I supposed to get through this?"

A lone sea gull's scream was the only answer.

"You're sure you'll be okay?" Spencer's fingers fumbled to fasten the tie at his neck as he stepped past a screaming Jonah. He tried to ignore the knot of panic in his stomach. The funeral started in half an hour, but how could he leave his brother alone with the twins, who'd been in a howling fit all morning?

"I'll be fine." Tyler bent to scoop a toy car out of Jeremiah's mouth, setting up another round of yells. "I'm their father. I have to learn to do this on my own at some point."

Tyler shoved Spencer's hands away from the tie, taking over for him. "I'm more worried about you."

"Me?" Spencer pretended not to know what his brother was talking about.

"Seriously, Spencer. You've always worn your heart on your sleeve. Just don't hand it over too easily. I know you care for this woman."

Spencer opened his mouth to argue, but Tyler cut him off. "If you didn't, you wouldn't have spent last night telling me every detail of every time you've seen her since she's been back."

Yeah, Spencer had known that would come back to bite him.

"I'm just saying—" Tyler cinched the knot around Spencer's neck. "Be there for her, but not *too* there. Her feelings are probably all mixed up right now. What might seem like affection is probably just her dealing with her own stuff from her grandma's death."

Spencer nodded. Tyler was right. He knew he was. But that didn't change the fact that he was determined to help Sophie through this. It's what friends did for each other.

With a last glance over his shoulder at the screaming twins, Spencer dashed out the front door.

Fog clung to him as he jogged to his truck. He'd be pushing it to get there in time.

He leaned forward in his seat to peer through the fog and spent the drive praying that he'd know how to offer Sophie the comfort she needed. She'd managed to hold back her tears at her grandma's bedside the other day, just as she always had, but he knew how much she must be hurting. It shredded him to think of her suffering like that alone. But that was Sophie. Even when they were dating, she'd never let him in completely.

He'd spent nearly every moment of the three days since her grandmother died fighting down the urge to call her, to burst into her parents' house and be there for her. He'd had to remind himself about a billion times that it wasn't his role anymore. But no matter how many times he repeated it to himself, he couldn't simply stop caring about her. Couldn't shut off the way his heart ached to be there for her.

*Well, you have to.*

Sophie wasn't his anymore. She had a new life. A new boyfriend. A new support system.

She'd only let Spencer comfort her the other day because he was the only one there.

The fog grew thicker as he got closer to the water, and Spencer had to slow almost to a crawl. But his thoughts were clearer than they'd been since Sophie returned. He pulled into the church parking lot with a new resolve. He'd go to the service, pay his respects, and then say goodbye and not think about Sophie again.

His plan steeled his steps as he exited the truck and strode toward the church. He could do this.

Inside, Sophie's parents stood at the front of the church, receiving the last few people waiting to offer their condolences. Spencer's eyes roved the crowded church, but he couldn't pick out Sophie's golden hair. He spotted Violet sitting near the back.

He moved to her and leaned down to whisper, "Where's Sophie?"

"I don't know." Violet shifted to make room for him. "I haven't seen her yet. Her mom said she went to get some water, but that was a while ago." Worry hovered in her eyes. "Maybe I should go find her."

Spencer stood. "I'll help."

As they opened the doors to step into the lobby, the pianist began to play "How Great Thou Art."

"We have to hurry." Violet pushed him into the lobby. "Sophie wouldn't want to miss this."

Actually, Spencer was pretty sure that's exactly what Sophie wanted. Whenever things became emotionally difficult, she ran.

"You check the bathrooms." He was already striding toward the long hallway off the lobby. "I'll see if she's in one of the conference rooms."

Violet nodded and sped in the opposite direction.

Spencer's thoughts skipped over all the places Sophie might have found to take refuge from her feelings. But as he passed a side exit, his eyes tracked to the beach, barely visible through the fog, and he knew.

He shoved out the door and charged down the rickety stairs that led to the beach below. He found her abandoned shoes at the bottom and scanned the sand in both directions. A smudged figure stood at the edge of the water a hundred yards down the beach. Spencer kicked off his shoes and set off toward her at a run. But he'd only covered half the distance between them when he started to question himself. Wasn't this exactly the kind of thing he'd just promised himself not to do? He slowed to a walk. She hadn't noticed him yet. He could turn around and walk away. Let her grieve in peace. Deal with things in her own way. It was what she'd want anyway.

He stopped, a collision of indecision, longing, and fear making it impossible to move.

At that moment, she glanced over her shoulder. Her hair swept around her face, making her look young and vulnerable. But it was the bleakness in her eyes that made his decision for him.

His steps devoured the distance between them, and he crushed her to him. She stiffened for a second, then sank into him. He breathed in the strawberry scent of her hair. He could stand like this forever.

But they didn't have forever.

After a few seconds, he moved his hands to her arms and gently nudged her back a step. "What are you doing out here, Soph? The service is about to start."

As if on cue, the church bells began to ring behind him.

Sophie winced and turned toward the smear of water and sky. In the fog, it was impossible to tell where one started and the other ended.

"I can't do it again." Her lips barely moved as she spoke.

Understanding washed over Spencer. How had he not realized it earlier? All of this must be bringing back so many memories. "Jordan?"

She flinched at his name. In all the years he'd known Sophie, she'd only talked about her brother a handful of times.

"I feel like the day we—" She bit her lip, and he was afraid she'd shut him out as she had so many times before.

But after a second, she continued. "The day we buried him, something broke in our family. My dad kind of checked out. And my mom—" A shiver shook her frame, and Spencer shrugged out of his suit coat and draped it over her shoulders. She pulled it tighter around herself but didn't look at him. "She was so angry. I think she turned off her feelings that day. And I'm afraid—" A wisp of hair fluttered onto her cheek, and Spencer automatically reached to tuck it behind her ear. She closed her eyes for a second, and he jerked his hand away. What was he thinking?

"You're afraid?" His voice came out hoarse.

Sophie sighed deep and long, the sound mimicking the brush of the waves against the beach. "I'm afraid maybe I turned off my feelings, too. And now, with all of this—" She gestured toward the church. "It's like they're trying to turn back on and—"

Spencer waited, barely breathing. She'd never been this open with him before.

"And it hurts," she finished in a whisper.

"Ah, Soph." It wrecked him to see her like this. But maybe it was what she needed. "It's not bad to feel." She opened her mouth—surely ready to protest—but he didn't let her get a word in. "I'm not saying it's always pleasant. But that hurt you feel? That's only because you felt so much love for her." The same reason he'd been so destroyed when Sophie had left him. He pushed the thought aside. "And if you let yourself feel that hurt now, it will get better someday. You'll be able to heal. But if you don't—if you keep trying to run from those feelings, they'll catch up with you eventually. And it will be so much harder."

Her eyebrows lowered, and she opened her mouth, looking ready for a fight. Spencer held up his hands to fend off the tirade. But instead of an argument, a strangled sob escaped her. She covered her mouth and turned away from him. But in a second, he'd spun her back around and pulled her close.

"It's okay." He stroked her hair. "You can cry. It's okay."

The sobs rocked her body, and all he could do was hold on and repeat that it was okay, that he was there.

When her tears finally slowed, he leaned back a fraction.

"I don't think your grandma would have wanted you out here, alone, thinking about how sad you are. She'd want you to be in there, celebrating that she's in heaven."

"Now you sound like her." A slight smile lifted the edges of Sophie's lips, and it was all he could do not to lean down and kiss them.

He dropped his arms. "Should we go inside?"

She blew out a long breath. "Will you stay with me?"

The gash in Spencer's heart deepened.

There was no way he could say no.

He held out a hand, and she grasped it, letting him lead her toward the stairs. As they stopped to put on their shoes, she studied him.

Her eyes were clouded, and he had no idea what she was thinking. "What?"

"Just— Thanks." She ducked her head and swiped at her eyes again. They were darker now, as if letting out all her feelings had deepened them. "That's the second time that you've come after me when I tried to run away."

Spencer wanted to say, "You're welcome," but his throat had closed off. He may have come after her these two times, but they couldn't make up for the one time he'd let her go.

# Chapter 14

Sophie clutched Spencer's hand as he opened the church door. The final strains of a hymn faded, and Sophie had to resist the urge to turn around and run. Spencer squeezed her hand and offered an encouraging smile. She drew in a breath and stepped through the doorway, Spencer right behind her. What would she do without him right now? And how had she come to rely on him so thoroughly when she'd promised herself that would never happen again?

"Oof." Sophie gasped as she was tackled in a hug.

"Oh, thank goodness." Vi gave her another squeeze, then released her. "You okay?" Her eyes traveled to where Sophie's hand was locked with Spencer's. Sophie gave a short nod and followed Vi to a seat near the back of the church, ignoring the curious looks directed her way. She clung tighter to Spencer's hand as they sat.

Pastor Zelner was just standing to deliver his message. "I knew Alice Harris almost my entire life. Whenever there was a potluck, I made sure she was going to be there. She made the best cakes." He patted his rounded stomach, and there was a smattering of laughter in the congregation. "Alice was an accomplished pianist. An avid boater. She was kind. Generous almost to a fault. She donated that beautiful playground we have outside. When she was younger, she gave her time to mission trips in Thailand. And when she couldn't physically make those journeys anymore, she provided funding so that others could." Pastor Zelner paused, letting his eyes travel the congregation.

Sophie's heart swelled with pride at all Nana had accomplished. She'd been a remarkable lady. Sophie only hoped she could accomplish half as much in her life.

"But—" Pastor Zelner picked up, and Sophie's eyes trained on him. "None of that matters."

Sophie shifted, ready to flee again. She wasn't going to sit here and listen to Pastor Zelner tear down everything Nana had done. Treat it as worthless.

But Spencer squeezed her hand and gave her a significant look.

*Fine.*

Back stiff, she focused her attention on Pastor Zelner, who continued, "And Alice would have been the first one to tell you that life wasn't about anything she was or anything she did or anything she achieved or gave. She knew that without Jesus, we are all worthless in God's sight."

Out of the corner of her eye, Sophie could see Spencer nodding. But she wanted to stand up and argue. If her achievements were worthless, what was the point of anything she'd done?

"But here's the thing Alice knew." Pastor Zelner's gaze roamed the church until it fell on her. Sophie stared back, daring him to go on.

"She knew her worth was in Christ alone." He shot her a gentle smile, then moved toward the other side of the church, letting his eyes sweep over the people. "The last time I met with Alice, she knew the end was near. And though she was sad to leave her family behind, she knew with absolute certainty where she was going. She told me there was one thing she wanted me to tell you all at her funeral. And if you knew Alice, you know that if she asked you to do something, you were going to do it." Sophie couldn't help but smile a little. He was right about that.

"So here's her message: You will never be enough on your own." Pastor Zelner's eyes locked right on hers—this time she was sure of it. Nana had probably orchestrated that. "But that's okay. Because you don't need to be enough. God doesn't care what you've accomplished. He loves you without condition. When you look to Christ, you will triumph. You will have everything. You will have the victory." He paused. "Just like Alice."

Sophie stood mechanically with the rest of the congregation, joined in singing the next song, bowed her head for prayer, but in the back of her mind, she kept hearing those words: *Look to Christ. Victory.*

Was it really that simple?

"Soph?" Spencer nudged her. "The service is over."

Sophie shook herself and glanced around. The church had largely emptied already.

She let Spencer pull her to her feet and lead her to the lobby, Vi following behind with a hand on Sophie's back.

In the lobby, Vi engulfed her in another hug. "I have to get back to the store, but let's get together before you leave."

Sophie startled. She hadn't even thought about returning to Chicago over the last few days. But there was really no reason to stay now. She nodded to Vi.

Seeming satisfied, Vi walked toward the doors but then looked back. "I mean it, Soph. Don't leave without telling me." Under the teasing note, Sophie heard the fear. She wouldn't do that to her friend again.

Sophie scanned the lobby, feeling lost. She was supposed to go bury Nana now, but she wasn't sure she could face that. Not alone.

She leaned toward Spencer to ask if he'd come with her. He'd already given her more than she deserved. She knew that. But she wasn't sure how else she could get through it.

"Hey, Spencer."

The eyes that fell on her were warm and open, and she stumbled. "I know I have no right to ask, but—"

"There you are." Her mother's call pulled their gazes across the lobby. Sophie turned in time to watch her close the last few feet to reach them, her lips set in a thin line, eyes dry, makeup perfect.

How could the woman be so composed when she was about to bury her own mother?

Mom's mouth tipped into a frown as her eyes fell on Spencer. Sophie could almost see her cataloging him: off-the-rack suit, bargain shoes, worn tie. The frown deepened as her eyes landed on their linked hands.

Instinctively, Sophie drew hers back. She couldn't deal with both Spencer and her mother right now. And this was the easiest solution. Even if the hurt in Spencer's eyes made her feel sick.

"Mom." She tried to keep her voice steady. "This is Spencer. We—" Oh, boy. How did she finish that sentence? "We went to college together."

Next to her, Spencer stiffened, but he held out a hand to her mother. "I'm sorry for your loss, Mrs. Olsen."

Her mother accepted his handshake about as eagerly as she would have taken a dried fish.

The moment she dropped it, she turned to Sophie. "The limousine is waiting to take us to the cemetery."

"Oh." She hadn't known there'd be a limo. Being confined in a car—no matter how luxurious—with her parents was the last thing she could handle right now. "Actually, I was just about to ask Spencer if he could—"

"It's okay, Soph." Spencer's voice was detached, and he refused to meet her eyes. "I should get back to help Tyler with the boys. And you should be with your family."

A crack opened right in her middle, and she wrapped her arms around her shoulders to keep her feelings from spilling out all over the floor. "Of course." She wasn't sure if the words actually came out or if she only thought them.

"Goodbye, Soph." With a last look she couldn't read, he disappeared through the doors.

And she wondered: Was this how he'd felt when she'd walked away?

# Chapter 15

Even the twins' giggles as they zigzagged between the trees couldn't touch the cold spot in Spencer's core that refused to thaw despite the sweat trickling down the front of his shirt.

"Uncle Spencer, can't get us," Jonah taunted from behind him.

Spencer shot the boys a half-hearted smile and made a vague gesture as if to chase them, but the twins weren't buying it. He didn't blame them. He wasn't buying it either.

"Un-cle Spen-cer." Jeremiah had sure perfected the art of whining.

"Leave your Uncle Spencer alone." Tyler wrestled a dead branch out of the tree they'd been pruning. "He's a grumpy pants today." Behind the funny voice, Spencer detected the note of I-told-you-so.

"Sorry, boys." He shook himself. "I'm not a grumpy pants. Just thinking."

About how Sophie had dropped his hand in front of her Mom yesterday. How she'd introduced him as a college classmate. She'd apparently never told her parents about their relationship.

He'd always suspected she'd rejected his proposal because she was ashamed of him.

Now he knew.

*That's her problem.*

He had plenty of other things to worry about. Like getting the rest of these trees pruned before they reached full bloom. And helping his brother move on with his life. And keeping his nephews entertained.

He set his clippers down. "Watch out, the tickle monster is coming." He wiggled his fingers at them and roared. The laugh that burst out of him as his nephews shrieked surprised even him.

He let himself forget everything else as he chased the boys, catching first one and then the other and tickling them until they were overcome with deep belly giggles. Finally, Tyler joined in and tackled him. Spencer struggled to escape his brother's pin as the boys set to tickling him.

Jeremiah got a hand in Spencer's armpit, and Spencer's howl set them all to laughing.

Spencer's heart swelled. This was what he'd longed for when he'd come back to the farm. Family. Warmth. Fun.

Over the last few years, the financial hits, the constant work and worry, had taken their toll, but if that's what it had taken to get to this point, it had all been worth it.

A strange sound cut through their fun, and they all paused.

"What's that?" Jonah's eyes were wide.

The noise sounded again. "It sounds like it's coming from under you." Tyler pointed through Spencer.

"It's my phone." Spencer tried to roll to the side. "Get off me, you oaf." He gave his brother a shove, then reached to grab his phone out of his back pocket.

"What's up, Violet?" With Cade gone, he'd become the one she relied on when she needed to move big pieces to her shop floor.

"Hey, I was just thinking—"

Spencer held back a sigh. Violet's "just thinking" usually ended up with him on a terrible blind date with someone she'd met who would be "perfect" for him. Problem was, he'd already met the woman who was perfect for him—only she didn't want anything to do with him.

"Sophie's leaving tomorrow after church," Violet continued, "and I thought it'd be fun if we all got together before she goes. We're going to meet at Sylvester's, okay? Seven o'clock. You have to come." She crammed it all into one breath, probably knowing he'd interrupt her to say no if she gave him even a split second.

Spencer hated to say no to Violet, no matter what she asked. Which is how he'd ended up on so many awful blind dates. But this was asking too much. Seeing Sophie when he knew he couldn't be with her. Knowing how she really felt about him. Saying goodbye to her all over again.

"I'm sorry, Violet, I don't think—"

"Please, Spencer." Her voice went up. "I need her to know she's welcome to come back. In the future. I don't want her to stay away five years again. Or longer. I've missed her."

So did he. Too much. Which is why he should say no and hang up right now.

But his traitorous mouth made the decision for him. "Fine. I'll see you at seven."

# Chapter 16

Sophie groaned as she pushed her plate away.

Across the table, Vi grinned at her. "Yeah, the Hidden Cafe has a way of making you eat way too much."

That was an understatement. The pile of fries on her plate had been stacked taller than her burger. And she'd eaten every last one.

But even better than the food had been the chance to reconnect with Vi. She'd done the right thing, giving in to Vi's plea that she stay for the weekend and head back to Chicago tomorrow afternoon.

She sighed. "This was great, but I should get back to my parents' to pack."

Vi tossed her napkin on the table and rummaged in her purse. "Oh, no, you don't. You're mine for the night, remember? We're going to Sylvester's."

"Sylvester's?" She couldn't hold back the surprised laugh. "Aren't we a little old for mini golf?"

Vi brushed off her argument and dropped some money on the table, then led the way to the door. "Never too old for mini golf. Anyway, we used to go all the time in college, if you remember."

But remembering was what Sophie was afraid of. All those trips to the mini golf course just blocks from campus. The way she'd pretended not to know how to putt, so Spencer would put his arms around her and help her. How they'd been mini golfing when he'd first asked if she'd consider going on a date with him. The way he'd ducked his head as he'd asked but then couldn't resist giving her a hug when she said yes.

"I'm sorry, Vi, but—"

"Nope," Vi cut in, steering her to the car. "You disappeared on me for five years. Tonight I get to decide what we do."

"Fine." Sophie let her head fall onto the headrest of the passenger seat. "But that's the last time you get to play that card tonight."

"Deal." For the one hundredth time, Sophie was overcome with gratitude at how easily her friend had forgiven her—she'd welcomed Sophie back into her life as if Sophie hadn't completely abandoned her for nearly half a decade.

As they got closer to Sylvester's, Vi tapped her finger against the wheel. Then she started bouncing her left leg. When she began to shoot surreptitious glances her way, Sophie threw up her hands. "What's going on, Vi?"

"Don't be mad." Vi's fingers drummed like mad on the steering wheel.

"Why would I be mad?" Sophie shifted in her seat to face her friend.

"There might be a few other people meeting us there."

"That's fine. You know—" But the realization hit her hard in the center of the chest. "Vi, no. I can't."

"Please." Vi turned down the street leading to Sylvester's. "You've been gone—"

Sophie held up a hand to stop her. "You just promised not to play that card again."

Vi laughed. "Fine. I won't." But she pulled into the driveway of the mini golf course and jumped out of her seat as if the matter had already been decided.

Sophie twisted Nana's ring around her finger. Either she sat in the car and looked like an idiot, or she got out and acted like an adult who could handle seeing her ex without going to pieces.

The first option seemed better all the time. But just when she'd decided to stay put, a familiar truck pulled into the space next to her.

Spencer gave her a grim not-quite-smile as he pushed open his door and climbed out. Before she knew what he was doing, he'd opened her car door, too.

She sat frozen for a moment, feeling suddenly exposed, as if he could read every thought of longing she'd had for him since he walked away yesterday.

"You coming?" Spencer's voice was bland, emotionless.

Fine. If he could do this, so could she.

They joined Vi in front of her car.

"Who else is coming?" Sophie tried to keep her voice even, despite the fact that standing so close to Spencer had set her stomach flip flopping.

"Ariana and Ethan are hoping to come, but she texted a little while ago to say we should start without them. Ethan got called to an accident, and it's hard to say when he'll be back." Vi linked her arm through Sophie's.

"What about Emma?" Not that she really wanted to know.

"She teaches riding lessons on Saturday nights." Spencer ran a hand over his face.

So it was just going to be the three of them. Sophie swallowed. That was fine. As long as she had Vi, everything would be fine. She wouldn't be tempted to do anything stupid. Like reach over to brush at the errant lock of hair that had fallen onto Spencer's forehead.

Sophie forced herself to look away as they got into line.

But she could feel Spencer behind her, and nothing could block out the welcoming, woodsy scent that always clung to him, as if he'd spent his whole day among the trees.

Which he probably had.

Sophie tried to take short, shallow breaths so she wouldn't become intoxicated from being so close to him. As soon as they had their clubs, she burst through the door leading to the course, leaving Vi and Spencer to grab the balls and scorecards. She sucked in a lungful of the popcorn-tinged air.

There, that was better.

Her head was clearer now.

"You okay?" Vi held out a ball and scorecard as she approached.

Sophie nodded. She was fine.

Absolutely fine.

But then Spencer came out of the building, his white button-down shirt failing to hide his broad shoulders, and she had to admit it. She was far from fine.

"We ready?" He didn't look at either of them.

"Yep." Vi's voice was overly cheerful as her eyes darted from Spencer to Sophie and back again. Obviously, things were not going according to her plans.

*Well, serves her right.*

Vi may have been responsible for getting them together in college, but that was a long time ago. Things had changed, and even Vi's matchmaking talents weren't up to this task.

They moved toward the first hole, but before they reached it, Vi's phone rang. Relief crossed her face as she pulled it out of her pocket. "It's Ariana. I'm sure they're on their way." She lifted the phone to her ear. "Hey, Ari. What's up?" She listened for a second. "Just a sec. I have terrible reception." She pulled the phone down and turned to Sophie and Spencer. "I'll be right back. You guys go ahead and play."

"We can wait for you. Actually, I'll come with you." No way was Sophie going to stay here alone with Spencer. That would be far too dangerous for her heart.

But Vi waved her away. "No. Go ahead. Otherwise we'll get stuck behind all these people." She pointed to the crowd that was starting to gather behind them. "Seriously, I'll be right back."

"Fine." Spencer shrugged and dropped his ball on the first green.

Sophie pressed down the welling panic as Vi walked away. If she didn't know better, she'd think her friend shot her a parting grin.

"Your stroke." Spencer's voice from behind made her jump.

*Get it together.*

She dropped her ball onto the artificial grass and surveyed the obstacles. There was a mini construction gate, complete with a "Caution" sign, about halfway down the course. She had to grimace at the irony.

"A little to the left." Spencer crouched at the other end of the green, studying the angle of her ball.

She shifted automatically, realigning her shot.

"Little more."

She shifted again.

"Just a tad more."

Sophie huffed and whacked the ball without moving again.

It sped toward the caution sign and hit it with a sharp thwack, ricocheting off and coming to a stop an inch from where it had started.

To his credit, Spencer didn't say anything.

He just tapped his ball into the hole and then waited silently as Sophie took three more strokes to get past the gate.

"Six," she said as the ball at last dropped into the hole.

"Not bad." Spencer's politeness irked her. Once upon a time, he'd have teased her for her lack of coordination, made fun of her impatience. As much as she'd always pretended to hate the teasing, she'd take it any day over this stiff formality.

She bent to pick up her ball, then jogged to catch up with Spencer, who was already halfway to the next hole. Vi had better get back soon. The two of them obviously couldn't handle being alone together much longer.

Thankfully, Vi reappeared just then. "Sorry about that. Ariana is having car trouble, so I told her I'd go pick her up."

Relief and disappointment washed over Sophie in equal measure. This might be the last time she ever saw Spencer, and she wasn't ready to say goodbye. And yet, spending more time together was clearly going to be unbearable.

She picked up the ball she'd been about to putt. "Let's go."

But Vi shook her head. "No, no. You two keep playing. I'll go get Ari."

"But Vi—"

But Vi had already done a quick pirouette and was bustling toward the exit. "We already paid," she called over her shoulder. "And you guys already started. Just keep going."

She disappeared into the crowd swarming outside the clubhouse. A second later, Sophie's eyes tracked her as she emerged on the other side of the building and practically ran through the parking lot to her car.

Behind her Spencer let out an exasperated laugh. "Classic Violet."

"What?" Sophie turned her gaze to him.

His brows were drawn low over his eyes, but the ghost of a smile hovered on his lips. "Remember the first time I asked you out?"

Of course she remembered.

They'd been at the mini golf course near campus, the three of them, and Vi had left to pick up Cade, who'd run out of gas and—

*Oh.*

"You don't really think she'd . . ."

But it didn't take his emphatic nod to tell her what she already knew. Of course she would. Just like she had that first time. She hadn't admitted until a year later that Cade hadn't run out of gas—that he was actually waiting for her down the block.

"She seems to like to play bad romantic comedy with our lives." Spencer twirled his golf club in his hands, and Sophie couldn't help the laugh that escaped. At least he was talking to her like a friend again. Not like the cold stranger who'd been filling in for him since he said goodbye at Nana's funeral yesterday.

But Vi's matchmaking still didn't make sense. "Why, though? I mean, it seemed like she and Emma are friends."

Spencer's eyebrows dropped into a V, and his forehead wrinkled. "They are. What does that have to do with anything?"

She hesitated. Maybe it'd hit a nerve, hearing his old girlfriend ask about his new one. "Well, I mean—"

"Excuse me?" A teen from the large group behind them cut in. "Are you going to play?"

"Why don't you putt through?" Spencer offered, stepping off the green and grabbing Sophie's elbow to tug her to the side with him. Now, more than ever, she had to ignore the jolt his touch sent through her.

"You were saying?" Spencer watched the group of teens, but his comment was definitely directed to her.

He was really going to make her say it.

*Fine.*

She kept her gaze directed at the teens, too. One of the boys was talking earnestly to a girl, who moved in closer, her eyes never leaving his face. Had that been them once?

"Well, I just think it'd be weird for Vi to recreate our setup when she likes Emma, and you two are clearly—" Did she really have to say the rest?

But Spencer was watching her now, his forehead even more creased. "Are clearly what?"

"Are clearly happy together." And in love. But she couldn't say that part.

She twisted her hands together, picking out the spots where her fingers interlocked.

Spencer's abrupt laugh made her head jerk up. "I guess we're as happy as two friends can be. But we're not together."

The pressure on Sophie's chest eased, but Spencer's look grew darker. "Of course, that doesn't excuse Vi for trying to set us up when you have a boyfriend."

Sophie stopped him with a hand on his arm. Suddenly it seemed important to set the record straight. "Chase isn't my boyfriend. He's a colleague."

Spencer's jaw relaxed.

But she wanted to be completely honest with him. "We did date a few times—"

Under her hand, Spencer's arm muscles went taut.

"But—" She forced herself to meet his eyes. "He wasn't right for me. I told him it was over when he was here."

"Yeah." Spencer shuffled away, and she let her hand fall to her side. "I hear women hate those good-looking, wealthy types."

"They may make good business partners, Spencer. But not—" She pushed the words out in a rush. "But not good life partners."

Spencer's eyes locked on hers. She could read the question in them. What kind of man would make a good life partner?

*You.*

But she didn't have a right to tell him that. She'd given up that right when she walked out on him.

The silence stretched between them, but neither looked away. "Soph—" Spencer's voice was quiet, tender.

"You guys can play now."

Sophie jumped, and Spencer's eyes flicked from hers to the kid who had interrupted them.

"Uh, we're done, so . . ." The kid scurried away at Spencer's scowl.

Spencer ran a hand through his hair, making it stick up on one side. A second ago, Sophie wouldn't have hesitated to smooth it. But now—

Now the spell had been broken.

And it was probably for the best.

"Should we golf?" Spencer gestured to the green, and Sophie shrugged. Vi had already paid for it. And she and Ariana should be here any minute.

Surely she could guard her heart until then.

# Chapter 17

"Eight." Spencer smirked as he jotted the number on Sophie's scorecard, and she shoved his shoulder playfully. Dark had fallen twenty minutes ago, and with it, everything that stood between them seemed to have fallen away as well. They were acting like the teens in front of them, trading teasing barbs and the occasional good-natured swat. It was like, while they were here at Sylvester's, the rest of the world, the rest of time, didn't exist. Life was simple, as it had been once. Neither of them had other responsibilities, other lives to get back to. All they had to worry about was this moment.

"Last one." Spencer led the way to the final hole, with the waterfall it was almost impossible to putt through. But going around took twice as many putts on a good day.

"Already?" The surprise in Sophie's voice delighted him. "I wonder what ever happened to Vi and Ariana."

Spencer gaped at her. He'd been having so much fun he'd forgotten that Violet and Ariana were supposed to join them. Hopefully they were okay.

But Sophie had pulled out her phone and was laughing.

"What?"

"Let's just say you were right. Definitely a setup." She passed him the phone, which was open to a text from Violet.

*Have fun!* Below that was a picture of Violet and Ariana waving—from Violet's kitchen.

"Those stinkers." He'd wanted to wring Violet's neck when she'd first pulled her disappearing act, but now he was ready to pick her up and twirl her around to thank her.

He passed the phone back to Sophie. "So how do you want to play this?"

Sophie studied him, apparently weighing his meaning. Finally, she shook her head. "You first." She gestured to the hole.

Okay. He could go along with that. Pretend there hadn't been more than the game behind his words.

He dropped his ball to the green and nudged it into position with his toe. He lined up his shot, and the ball banked off the wall, in perfect position to go around the waterfall on his next shot.

He gave a mock bow, but Sophie raised an eyebrow. "Playing it safe?"

"Sometimes that's the best way to get to your goal." Something it had taken him a long time to learn.

He took his next two shots, then sunk the ball in the hole on the fourth. He waited as Sophie lined up her shot. Her hair hung in her face, and she paused to grab a rubber band off her wrist and pull it into a ponytail. The casual hair, combined with the pink shirt, slim jeans, and tennis shoes, made her look like a softer version of herself, more open. More kissable.

The thought popped into his head, and once it was there, he couldn't erase it.

Didn't want to, really.

Sophie lifted her eyes at that moment and caught him staring at her. He should look away, pretend he hadn't been watching her. But he didn't.

She gave him a slow smile, and he was pretty sure his heart stopped for a beat.

She tucked a loose hair behind her ear, then dropped her head, swung the putter, and gave the ball a sound whack.

"And sometimes you have to take a risk." Her eyes followed the ball as it sailed toward the waterfall. It hit the wall of spray with a thud, and Sophie ran to his side to watch as it sailed through the waterfall. The momentum of the spin pulled it toward the hole.

Sophie clutched his arm. "Keep going. Keep going." She bounced on her toes.

With a clatter, the ball dropped into the hole.

"Yes!" Before he could react, she had thrown her arms around him.

All the air whooshed out of him in surprise, but his arms rose to her back of their own accord.

She felt so good.

He could get used to this again. He could—

*No you can't.*

Gently, he let go.

After a second, Sophie seemed to come to her senses and let go, too.

"Sorry." But her cheeks were flushed an adorable pink, and her eyes held a light he hadn't seen the whole time she was home. "That was fun."

He nodded as he led the way to the clubhouse. It had been fun, and he hated that it was over. He wanted to live in this time warp forever. But that wasn't how life worked.

Inside, they placed their clubs on the counter and turned to leave, but the clerk stopped them. "Don't you want to play the second round your friend paid for?"

Spencer's eyes met Sophie's, and he was pretty sure his own face mirrored the grin on hers. Maybe, just for tonight, they could stay in this time bubble.

An hour later, Spencer's cheeks hurt from smiling so much. A small price to pay for such a fantastic evening.

He hadn't had such a good time since—

Well, since he and Sophie had been together.

"I really think I improved my score that time." Sophie bent to grab her ball out of the final cup. Spencer snorted, and she stood to elbow him. "Except for the last hole."

He snorted again. It'd taken her fifteen strokes on the final hole this time. The ball had bounced off the waterfall on the first fourteen attempts, but she'd insisted it would be more satisfying to go through the obstacle than to go around it. Spencer had to give her credit for that.

But not for her final score. He finished tallying. "So, your first round, you had one hundred eight. And this round . . ." He left a dramatic pause, enjoying the anticipation in her eyes too much. "One hundred thirty-six."

The laugh that burst out of her was the most delicious sound he'd ever heard.

"Oh, yeah, Mr. Showoff? And what was your score?"

"Fifty-one," he deadpanned.

She plucked the scorecard out of his hand and reviewed it. "Well, then it looks like you get to buy me ice cream."

He snorted again. But any excuse to spend more time with her was fine by him.

They dropped their equipment off, and he opened his truck door for her, still caught in the time trap of mini golf. How many times had he held a door for her, ushered her into his truck, taken her for ice cream?

The drive was quiet. But it wasn't the uncomfortable silence of earlier. It was the kind of pleasant quiet that flowed from knowing a person so well there was no need for words.

He had to park several blocks from the Chocolate Chicken. That's what happened when it was the only place on the peninsula open after ten. He jumped out of the truck and crossed to open her door. A sense of déjà vu overtook him as they walked next to each other. The only difference was they weren't holding hands this time. He resisted the urge.

Inside, Sophie leaned toward him. "I think we might be the old folks here."

Spencer surveyed the shop. Sure enough, it overflowed with young people in groups and couples. They appeared to be the oldest ones in the place. Apparently time had marched on after all. The room was warm and bright, the buzz of voices loud. "Want to take this to the gazebo?" Spencer passed her the double scoop of triple chocolate in a waffle cone.

Sophie nodded as she took her first lick. Spencer had eaten ice cream with her so many times before that he knew to watch for it—the way her eyes closed as she savored the first taste.

She gave him a sheepish grin as she opened her eyes again, then led the way to the door.

A cool breeze blew in off the lake as they made their way to the public gardens on the hillside above the marina.

A gust played with a strand of hair that had come loose from Sophie's ponytail, sweeping it across her face—and into her ice cream. She groaned.

"Just a sec." They'd passed his truck half a block ago, and Spencer jogged back to it. He grabbed a stack of napkins from the glove box, then, in a flash of inspiration, reached into the backseat to grab the blanket he always kept for emergencies.

A second later, he was at Sophie's side.

"You think of everything." She took the napkin he held out to her and wiped at the chocolate streak in her hair.

"You missed a little." Spencer pointed to the ice cream dripping off a strand of hair, careful not to get too close. Sophie swiped toward the spot with her napkin.

"That wasn't even close." He couldn't help the laugh.

"Well, then help me." Sophie thrust the napkin at him.

He swallowed, the laughter dying on his lips. To help her, he'd have to touch her, and if he touched her—

His pulse jumped at the thought.

"It's right"—he tried to do a more accurate job of pointing—"there."

But Sophie shook the napkin at him. He licked his suddenly too-dry lips and took it, passing her his ice cream.

The moment his hand fell on her silky hair, a flood of memories overtook him. Sitting on the park bench, letting her teach him to braid her hair. Absently combing through it with his fingers as they watched a movie. Sliding his hands into it as he kissed her.

His eyes darted to her lips, glistening with a faint trace of ice cream. He yanked his gaze back to her hair and concentrated on wiping at the sticky ice cream coating the strands.

"There." He forced himself to lower his hands. To take his ice cream. To act as if his heart hadn't just jumped out of his chest and thrown itself to the ground at her feet, ready for her to cradle it or stomp on it, as she pleased.

They strolled onto the path that led through the public garden toward the gazebo. Old-fashioned street lamps that could be straight out of a Dickens novel lined the path, casting patches of light and shadow on the tulips that had closed their petals for the night. The damp scent of the lake carried on the wind.

Next to him, Sophie sighed. "I didn't realize how much I missed this place."

"Yeah?" Her words hooked right into his heart, tugging at it.

They stepped into the gazebo and settled on a bench facing the water. He spread the blanket across both their laps. Sophie burrowed into it, pulling the worn fabric to her shoulders.

"I miss the gazebo. The ice cream. The lake." She hesitated, eyes directed toward the water. "The people."

He froze. *What people?*

But he didn't have the courage to ask.

Besides—

"Correct me if I'm wrong, but you have the same lake in Chicago."

Her eyes slid to him, and she stiffened.

"Come on, Soph, someone had to bring it up."

*What are you doing to me here?* his heart screamed. *If you hadn't brought it up—*

*What?* His common sense got the better of him. *She'd have forgotten she lives in Chicago and has her own life?*

Spencer tried to ignore the internal argument and forced his attention back to Sophie.

"It's not the same lake there," she was saying, her expression earnest. "I mean, technically, it's the same lake. But it's not the same, you know?"

He nodded. He did know. It was like how cherry trees that weren't part of Hidden Blossom were still cherry trees, but they weren't the same. Or how Sophie was the same as she'd been when she was his but not the same.

"Anyway." Sophie licked the last bits of ice cream from her fingers. "I almost never get out on the lake there. I'm always working."

Spencer could relate. "But you love what you're doing?"

She shrugged. "I'm up for a big promotion."

"That's great, Soph." But something between them had shifted when he'd brought up Chicago. He might as well deliver the final blow. "You go back tomorrow?"

Did a shadow of regret pass over her eyes, or was he only imagining it? "I head out after church."

He'd already known the answer, but his whole body tensed. What was he doing here, with the woman who'd already shattered him once? Who would only shatter him again when she drove away tomorrow?

But that wasn't fair. She hadn't come to Hope Springs to see him. She'd come to say goodbye to her grandma. She didn't owe him anything.

He couldn't take the way she was looking at him. "It's too bad you didn't get a chance to see the cherries blossom," he said, just to fill the silence. "They're starting to open."

"Maybe next time."

He nodded. But he knew there wouldn't be a next time. Once she left . . .

It'd likely be the last time he ever saw her.

"Spencer." His whispery-soft name on her lips almost undid him.

He let himself slide toward her. Let the soft dance of the moonlight on her lips beckon him closer.

He had dreamed of this moment for the past five years. But he'd never expected that dream to come to life.

*And once it did, then what?*

Who cared? He'd deal with that tomorrow. For now, all he wanted was this moment.

He slid a fraction closer, his eyes never leaving hers. He could read it there—she wanted the same thing.

But he couldn't shake the thought of her leaving.

He straightened and cleared his throat. "We should probably go. You have a long drive tomorrow." The words clawed their way out, leaving behind a raw trail that burned up his throat.

Sophie's eyes stayed on his a moment longer—long enough for him to glimpse the hurt there before a hood dropped over her expression.

"You're right." She got up in a quick motion that yanked the blanket off his lap.

But the sudden chill that cut through him had nothing to do with the cold air.

Sophie gathered the blanket into a ball, then took off down the garden path, leaving him to catch up.

# Chapter 18

The burning behind Sophie's eyes was nothing to the burning in her heart. She'd been reading Nana's journal for the past two hours, unable—or maybe unwilling was the better word—to turn out the lights and go to sleep. She was afraid of whose face would haunt her dreams if she did. Afraid she'd see the way he'd pulled back when she'd said she was leaving tomorrow. Afraid she'd feel the too-gentle squeeze he'd given her hand when he dropped her off at her parents'. Afraid she'd remember her own desire to kiss him—a desire that had almost overcome her common sense.

She shook her head. Here she was thinking about it again.

She turned back to Nana's journal. Reading Nana's words over the last days had filled her heart in a way nothing else ever had. Her grandmother had had an incredible faith—a faith that had survived through the death of her husband and grandson, through her daughter's rejection, through her granddaughter's abandonment. Through it all, Nana had never shown anything less than love for them all—and even more, for God. Her journal was full of Scripture verses Sophie had known once but hadn't thought about in years. Her favorite so far was from Romans: "But God demonstrates his own love for us in this. While we were still sinners, Christ died for us."

The sheer magnitude of that kind of unconditional love took Sophie's breath away. Christ had died for her while she was still a sinner. She hadn't done anything to earn or deserve his approval, and yet he approved her anyway because of Jesus.

It had gotten her thinking about Pastor Zelner's comments at Nana's funeral—about finding her worth in Christ. If God approved of her, what did it matter if she ever won the approval of her parents or her boss or even Spencer?

A giant yawn overtook her, and she closed her eyes, the journal still open on the bed next to her.

A strange heaviness clung to Sophie as she packed, making her movements lethargic.

She clicked on her phone to check the time.

Noon.

She should be on the road. Church had been done for an hour already.

She'd said her goodbyes to Vi and Ariana and Ethan there. Spencer had been conspicuously absent from the service, and she couldn't help but feel it was her fault. That he didn't want to see her one last time before she left.

As she clicked the phone off, she pretended not to notice the swoop of disappointment that he hadn't called or texted. She'd let herself half-hope he'd try to convince her to stay. But he hadn't the first time, so why should he now?

And anyway, it's not like she'd really consider staying. She couldn't. Her job, her life, was in Chicago.

Even if, over the past week and a half, it was like someone had taken all the appeal she'd felt for Chicago and flipped it to Hope Springs. Which was ridiculous. She hadn't been able to wait to escape this place.

But being back, seeing family, seeing friends, and, fine, seeing Spencer had reminded her what she'd given up when she left.

Finally, her suitcase was packed, and she had no more excuses to stall. She surveyed the room. Better not forget anything. Who knew when she'd be back.

Her eyes fell on the worn copy of *Pride and Prejudice* on the nightstand. She grabbed the book and flipped it open to the page with the cherry blossom. Her fingers traced the paper-thin petals.

She should leave it here. Then there'd be nothing to tempt her to think about Spencer.

Yeah, nothing but her memories. Ones she'd thought she'd buried long ago but that had fought their way to the front of her thoughts and refused to leave.

She snapped the book shut and tucked it into the front of her suitcase, then pulled the suitcase off the bed and wheeled it into the hall. The thought of talking to her parents was suddenly too much, but she couldn't just walk out without saying goodbye. A search of the kitchen, formal dining room, and living room came up empty. They'd come home with her after church, but apparently they'd taken off again. She suppressed a sigh. Why should she be surprised that they hadn't stuck around to see her off? Anyway, this would make things easier. Which didn't explain the pit in her stomach. Did they really care that little about her?

Whatever. She was done worrying about what they thought of her.

She forced her chin up and wheeled her suitcase toward the front door.

But as she passed the den, she paused. She could have sworn she heard a rustling sound from inside. But that didn't make sense.

Neither of her parents had been in that room in years, as far as she knew. Heart thundering, she crept to the doorway and peeked cautiously inside.

"Mom?" In her surprise, the word came out louder than she intended, and her mother's head jerked up. She lifted a quick hand to swipe at her eyes but not before Sophie saw the moisture hovering on her lashes. An old photo box sat open in front of Mom, but she dropped the picture she'd been examining and yanked the cover onto the box.

Shock coursed through Sophie, but she wasn't sure what startled her more—seeing Mom crying or seeing the photo box. She recognized it immediately.

"Are those—?" She stepped gingerly into the room, easing toward Mom.

"They're nothing." Mom twisted to stash the box in its spot under an unused stack of books on the built-in shelves, but Sophie intercepted her. With something approaching reverence, she lifted the cover off the box. After Jordan died, she'd pored through this box so many times, until Mom caught her and told her it was off limits. She said Sophie needed to move on and that dwelling on her brother would only hold her back from her own life.

Sophie only wished she'd understood then that Mom's way of dealing with grief was unhealthy, that ignoring your feelings wasn't an answer. She picked up the photo Mom had thrown on top of the pile.

It was one of her and Jordan, playing together in the lake. Mom had snapped the picture right as Jordan sent a huge splash of water careening toward Sophie. She was smiling in this picture, but the moment after, she'd been crying and screaming at Jordan.

What she wouldn't give to have moments like that again. "I miss him."

Mom's head swung toward her, and Sophie covered her mouth. She hadn't meant to say it out loud. She knew Mom wouldn't talk about him.

But Mom gave a tight nod. "Heading out?"

"You know, I think Nana managed to get a picture of me screaming at him after this. When she showed it to me, I asked if she was going to throw it away." Sophie kept talking as Mom moved toward the doorway. "She said we should keep it because it was important to remember all the moments—not just the good ones—because it's all the moments that make us who we are." Sophie had thought then that Nana was crazy, but now she was starting to understand what Nana had meant.

Sophie lifted her head. If Mom could only see, too. But Mom had disappeared down the hallway.

Sophie shook her head at herself. Why did she bother?

But for some reason she couldn't explain, she felt compelled to follow Mom to the kitchen.

She stood at the counter, waiting for Mom to pour herself a cup of coffee. The sag to Mom's shoulders unnerved Sophie almost as much as seeing her cry had. Since the day of Jordan's funeral, she'd never seen her mother anything less than one hundred percent put together.

She longed to step around the counter, hug Mom, and tell her they could mourn Jordan and Nana together. But they'd never had that kind of relationship.

She bit her lip, trying to figure out how to say goodbye.

But Mom beat her to it. "You should get going."

Sophie nodded and opened her mouth to agree, but instead, what came out was, "I could stay a little longer if you wanted."

Mom's eyes flicked to hers. "Why would I want you to stay?"

All the air seeped out of Sophie, like a balloon with a small hole that widens as it deflates. "Never mind," she mumbled. "Just thought you might need help cleaning out Nana's house." She reached for the handle of her suitcase.

"I called a service to do that. They should have everything out of there by the end of the week."

Sophie let go of the suitcase, wincing as it crashed to the floor. "What will they do with it all?"

Her mother took a slow sip of coffee. "What do you mean what will they do with it? They'll donate the furniture and stuff. Toss the rest."

Sophie pressed a fist to her stomach. Could her mother really let some strangers throw everything of her grandmother's away?

"Don't you want to keep anything?" Her voice sounded high and little-girlish, but she suddenly felt like a little girl.

"Of your grandmother's?" Mom may as well have rolled her eyes for how well she hid the scoff in her voice. "She decorated her house with garage sale bits and pieces. There's nothing worth anything there."

"What about her personal stuff? Jewelry, pictures?"

Sophie's mother drained her cup. "Your grandmother wore costume jewelry and took terrible pictures. None of it's worth keeping. It's just stuff. Junk."

Sophie supposed it was true that it was just stuff. But stuff could have meaning, couldn't it? Memories?

"What if I clean out the house?" The words came out before Sophie could think them through. "Or we could do it together."

Her mother studied her with the closest thing to compassion Sophie had seen from her in a long time. She didn't dare to breathe. Was Mom really going to say yes? But Mom's careful, neutral expression snapped back into place. "You have to get back to work. And I have better things to do with my time than sort through your grandmother's clutter."

Mom was right, of course. She did have to get back to Chicago. But the thought of every memory she'd made with Nana being thrown into the trash was too much. And besides, the moment the idea had popped into her head, she'd been overcome with a peace she hadn't known in a long time. She didn't know why exactly she felt the need to stay, but she did.

"It'll only take a few days. I haven't taken a single vacation in the five years I've been with the firm. I have plenty coming to me. I'll just call Chase and let him know."

Her mother raised an eyebrow. "Chase, the man who was here the other day?"

Sophie nodded warily. Here came another lecture.

"Good, and while you're talking, make sure you patch up whatever went wrong the other day. He certainly suits you better than that farmhand you sat with at your grandmother's funeral."

Sophie's chest burned, and she fought every instinct to lash back. Spencer wasn't a farmhand. He was running that farm. And whatever he chose to do with his life, he was the best man she'd ever known.

But there was no point in defending Spencer to her mother. It's not like she'd ever be with him again anyway.

"So you're okay with me cleaning out Nana's house?"

"If you can get it done in a week. I want to get that house on the market before tourist season is in swing. Lots of potential buyers then."

"Deal." Sophie snatched her suitcase and headed for her room to unpack, her footsteps lighter than they'd been since Nana died.

She dialed Chase's number, more than a little relieved when he didn't answer, and left a message that she needed to sort some things out and would be staying another week. She promised to make it up to him by dealing with their least favorite architect on every project for a year.

As she passed through the kitchen, she asked Mom one more time to come with her. Apparently, she was a glutton for punishment.

But at least her expectations were realistic enough that she wasn't crushed when Mom repeated her no.

On the way to the car, Sophie pulled out her phone.

Her finger hovered over the number for only a second before she pressed it. This time her expectations were too high. But she couldn't bring herself to dampen them.

# Chapter 19

Spencer slammed the stack of financial statements to the kitchen table and snatched at his ringing phone. He scowled at the unfamiliar number on the screen. He couldn't shake the bad mood that had clung to him all morning as he pictured Sophie on the road back to Chicago. It didn't help that since the moment he'd gotten home from church he'd been trying to deal with the farm bills that had piled up while Dad was in the hospital. Managing the books was his least favorite part of life on the farm, especially when a look at their financial standing left him wondering how they'd make it to harvest without going bankrupt.

"What?" he snarled into the phone. He was in no mood to be polite to telemarketers today.

"Spencer?"

Spencer closed his eyes, all the pent-up frustration leaking from him. In its place he was left with something even harder to handle.

Hope.

He tried to tamp it down.

"Hey, Soph. Is everything okay?" Maybe she'd gotten a flat tire or something on her way out of town.

"Yeah, everything's fine. I don't know why I called, actually. Well, I mean, I do, but I'm not sure why I thought you— I mean, I wanted to—"

Spencer couldn't help his grin. Sophie was always so certain, and yet, on the rare occasion when she wasn't, she babbled like a fool.

A very cute fool.

"What's up, Soph?"

He heard a quick intake of breath. "You weren't in church this morning."

He tapped his pen against the table in a sharp rhythm. "I went to church in Silver Bay this morning."

"Oh." How could she put so much meaning into one syllable?

"It's closer and—"

"Yeah, of course." Sophie brushed off his lame excuse. "Anyway, I was just calling to ask if your invitation to see the cherry blossoms was still good."

Spencer dropped the pen. "Aren't you going back to Chicago?"

"No. I mean, yes." Another quick breath. "I mean, I am, but not for a few more days. I'm staying to help clean out Nana's house first."

Spencer fought to control the way his heart surged. She was staying for a few more days. Not forever.

"So does it?" She sounded tentative, unsure, and he wanted to reassure her, tell her of course it did—whatever "it" was, but he couldn't for the life of him remember her question.

"Does it what?"

Her sparkling laugh reached right through the phone and wrapped itself around his heart. "Does the invite to see the cherries still stand?"

"Yeah." He pushed the words out past the snag of emotions. "It still stands."

"Great." Relief and something deeper mingled in her voice, but Spencer refused to let himself put a name to it. "I need to get a start at Nana's first, but how about I come around four?"

"Four sounds perfect." Spencer hung up and tried to focus on the paperwork in front of him. But it was hopeless. He shoved the papers aside and jammed his feet into his work boots. He needed to move.

On the way out the door, he almost bowled Tyler and the twins over.

"Hey." He swept Jonah up into a hug. "How's Grandpa?"

"Good." Jonah squirmed free and ran into the house, followed by Jeremiah.

Spencer looked to Tyler, waiting for his assessment.

"They're planning to release him later today." A giant smile overspread Tyler's face. "Our old man's one tough guy."

A relieved laugh made its way up from Spencer's core, and he pulled his brother in for a quick hug. "Thank the Lord." If Dad was coming home, then everything would be fine. He'd take over the paperwork, get everything squared away.

"By the way, Mom wants to have a celebration dinner tonight." Tyler gave him one last clap on the back and released him.

"Tonight?"

Tyler gave him a playful shove. "Yeah. Why, you have plans?"

Spencer shoved back. "Maybe."

Tyler's eyebrows shot up. "Really? I didn't think you'd get over Sophie that quickly. I *am* good."

Tyler may have been awake when Spencer got home last night. And Spencer may have poured his heart out to him. And Tyler may have helped him see that Sophie's leaving before he got his heart in any deeper was a good thing.

Spencer kicked one boot into the other. "Actually, the plans are kind of with Sophie. She called to say she's staying a couple more days to clean out her grandma's house. And she wanted to come see the cherry blossoms."

"Spencer, she's—"

Spencer held up a hand. "I know. She's going to leave. And I'm prepared for that."

"Really?" Tyler's eyebrows were so high they almost got lost in his hairline. "Is that why you about stuffed Jeremiah into the trash when he asked for a piggyback ride this morning?"

"I didn't—" But Spencer couldn't deny that he'd let his mood affect his interaction with his nephews this morning. "I'll go apologize."

Tyler grabbed his arm. "There's no need. He thought it was funny. It's just—"

Tyler peered past Spencer toward the orchard, but Spencer got the impression he was seeing farther, into the past. "I know how much it hurts to be left. And I may not have been there for you the first time. But I'm here now. And I don't want you to get hurt."

Spencer clapped a hand to his brother's shoulder. "I know what I'm doing. You don't have to worry about me."

Tyler rubbed at his forehead. "I'm the big brother. It's my job to worry."

Spencer didn't have the heart to remind him that for most of their adult lives he'd been the one to take on the big brother role. He appreciated Tyler's genuine concern.

"So anyway," Spencer said after a moment. "Do you think Mom and Dad will mind if I bring Sophie?"

"No." Tyler huffed. "You know Mom. Always the romantic. The last thing she told me when I left was to make sure you didn't let Sophie go this time."

Spencer spluttered. "Let her—? But she— I—"

Tyler lifted his arms and stepped into the house. "Take it up with Mom. She seems to think you two are meant to be together. Of course, she still watches fairy tales, too, so . . ."

Spencer joined his brother's laugh as he bounded down the steps and headed toward the workshop. But the truth was, he was beginning to agree with Mom.

If only Sophie was, too.

⸎

Anticipation coursed through Sophie as she turned into the driveway of Hidden Blossom Farms. It was because of the cherry blossoms, she told herself. It had nothing to do with the almost visceral need she'd felt to see Spencer again.

He was leaning against the shed when she pulled up, looking like he belonged in some outdoor magazine in his faded jeans and white t-shirt, hands perched easily in his pockets, dark hair rumpling slightly in the breeze. Sophie's grip on the wheel tightened, and her mouth went dry. This was a bad idea. Being here with him was only going to confuse her more. Make her want something she couldn't have.

But she couldn't hold back the smile that stretched her lips as soon as she stepped out of the car.

"Hey, Soph." She'd always loved the way he said her name. The way he lingered a moment on the "o."

"Hey, yourself." She drew in a deep breath of the blossom-tinted air. This was the scent of spring she'd been craving. A warm breeze lifted her hair, and she brushed it back. "It's so peaceful out here."

Spencer smiled and crossed the driveway to stand next to her. "How was your grandma's?"

"It was—" She paused before the word "fine" could slip out. She was determined to be completely open with him. "It was sad but good." Going through Nana's stuff had brought back wave after wave of memories. And even though it hurt that she wouldn't be able to make new memories with Nana, it had been comforting to think about all the memories she'd already collected.

"Actually." She opened the rear door of the car and leaned inside, reaching around Nana's favorite cookie jar—an ugly thing in the shape of a tree stump with a squirrel on top—that she couldn't bear to part with.

"This reminded me of you." She pulled her head out of the car and passed him the ship in a bottle that used to sit on top of Nana's bookshelf.

"Wow," Spencer breathed, lifting the tiny bottle to examine the intricate ship inside.

"I was thinking about that time we went to the museum, remember? And you stood and looked at that ship in a bottle for like twenty minutes."

He met her eyes. "I remember that day. It was the first time—"

He dropped his eyes back to the bottle. But he didn't need to say it. She remembered their first kiss, too.

It'd been dark by the time they'd emerged from the museum, and they'd been laughing about something stupid—Sophie couldn't remember what anymore. But when they stopped laughing, the air had seemed to shift around them. Spencer had grazed a hand lightly over her cheek, then leaned down and brushed the softest kiss onto her lips. When he'd pulled back, she'd tugged him closer for another, deeper kiss.

Sophie touched two fingers to her lips, remembering how it had been different from any other kiss she'd ever had. It had felt real. True. Life-changing.

She looked up at him now, and when their eyes met, she could almost pretend that the last five years had fallen away, that they were still together. That he still loved her.

But of course the years had happened. They weren't still together. He didn't still love her.

And she didn't still love him.

Obviously.

"See that?" Spencer pointed to something inside the bottle, and Sophie closed the space between them to get a better look.

"There." Spencer shifted so that his shoulder was pressed against hers. "See that fine detail, the carved dragon on the helm. Isn't it amazing?"

Sophie nodded, but the only details she could concentrate on were his hands, curved around the glass; his eyes, crinkling as he squinted at the ship; his arm, brushing against hers. And his scent—that fresh clean smell she'd missed so much.

"Anyway." Spencer held the bottle out to her. "Thanks for showing me this."

She shook her head and pushed it back to him. He'd always been so terrible at accepting gifts. "I want you to have it."

He gave her another doubtful look but closed his hand around it. "Why?"

"Because you like it. Because it makes you happy. Because I—" She broke off in confusion. She couldn't say the words that were about to roll off her tongue too easily. "I just want you to have it."

Spencer's eyes seemed to slip right past her defenses, see right into her heart.

He took a step back, clearing his throat. "Thank you. Let me put this in the house, and then I'll give you the tour."

As soon as he disappeared inside, Sophie pulled in a few deep breaths. She had to be more careful.

She wasn't staying indefinitely, and she was determined not to break his heart this time.

Even if it meant breaking her own.

# Chapter 20

Spencer set the ship in a bottle on a high shelf in the living room. As long as the twins didn't scale the shelf—which he couldn't entirely rule out—it would be safe.

He should get back out to Sophie, but he needed to collect himself. He couldn't read too much into the fact that she'd given him a gift from her grandma's house. Or the fact that she'd stayed in Hope Springs a few extra days. That she'd sought him out.

A burst of noise from outside pulled him to the door. He shoved it open as he caught sight of the chaos in the yard. The twins were chasing each other around Sophie's legs as Tyler tried to talk to her over their squeals. So much for peaceful.

"Jonah! Jeremiah!" He jogged across the lawn. "Here comes the tickle monster." If he caught their attention, hopefully they'd leave Sophie alone.

But they weren't interested in him.

"Boo!" Jonah waved his hands at Jeremiah as he took off around Sophie again.

Spencer scooped to pluck first Jonah then Jeremiah off the ground. The boys wiggled, but he firmed his grip, chancing a glance at Sophie. Amusement sparkled in her eyes, and a smirk played on her lips. Something inside him eased. She'd never hidden the fact that she didn't want children, but the way she was looking at these two . . .

*Whoa, there, buddy. Where you going with that thought?*

Right.

Enough of that.

"Now, boys, this is how we greet a lady." He shifted them to the ground and crouched beside them. "You hold out your right hand, like this." He stuck his hand out, waiting for the boys to mimic him.

"Good. Then you take her hand in yours, and you shake it, like this." He grasped Sophie's hand, ignoring the rough rhythm his heart took up. He pumped her hand gently twice, but he couldn't bear to let go quite yet. "And then"—he winked at the boys—"if you really want to be a gentleman and you really like her, you kiss her hand." He flipped Sophie's hand over in his and brought it gently toward his lips.

Behind him, Tyler cleared his throat. Loudly.

Spencer jumped and dropped Sophie's hand. He kept his head down.

"Now you try it." He gave Jonah a gentle push in front of him, practically using the boy as a shield.

Jonah shyly held out a hand, and Sophie crouched to take it. "It's nice to meet you." She shook Jonah's hand, but her eyes were locked on Spencer. He could feel it even though he hid his own gaze in Jonah's hair.

"Nice meet you," Jonah repeated woodenly, and they all laughed.

"Do you want to kiss her hand?" Spencer murmured to his nephew.

"Ew." Jonah wiggled away, but Jeremiah pushed into his spot. "Me turn."

He grabbed Sophie's hand and yanked it toward him, knocking her off balance.

Spencer's hand shot out to steady her, but Jeremiah kept pulling until her hand was at his mouth.

Instead of the quick peck Spencer had been about to demonstrate, Jeremiah dropped a big, juicy kiss right in the middle of Sophie's open palm.

Spencer flinched, but Sophie's laugh washed over them. "I see you have your uncle Spencer's way with women."

Spencer ignored Tyler's hearty guffaw at that.

"Hey, come here," Sophie whispered to Jeremiah. He shuffled a few steps closer, and she leaned over and dropped a quick kiss on his cheek. "You're quite the charmer."

He giggled, then ran off in the direction Jonah had gone, screaming that he was the kiss monster.

"Guess they learned a new game." Spencer straightened, pulling Sophie up with him.

"Great." But Tyler's eyes were directed pointedly at the spot where Spencer still gripped Sophie's elbow.

Spencer let go and crossed his arms in front of him.

Sophie turned to Tyler. "You have lovely boys."

Tyler groaned as the twins disappeared behind the house. "Not sure lovely is the word I'd use." But he took off after them with a smile.

"He's a good dad." Spencer couldn't help but be impressed with how well Tyler had adjusted to caring for the twins.

"I can tell." Sophie dropped a casual hand onto his arm. "He said your dad's coming home from the hospital today. That's such great news."

"Yeah." Spencer was caught up in the way her eyes gleamed. She was genuinely happy for his family, he could tell.

"I'm sure you want to be with him for that. We can do this another day." Sophie took a step toward her car.

He grabbed her arm to stop her. "He won't be home until later this afternoon. Actually, we're having a little celebration tonight—"

"Oh. Of course. I'm sure he'll—" She tried to pull away again.

"Soph." He didn't mean to sound so exasperated, but couldn't she see he was trying to tell her something? "I'd like it if you came to that. With me."

Her lips parted a little, and he had to fight down the temptation to kiss her right then and there.

"With you?"

He slid his hand down her arm to grasp her hand. "With me."

Hesitation hovered in her eyes.

"Please? For my dad? He won't stop talking about the lovely girl who brought him flowers. I mean, he knows your name, but he calls you that anyway. Lovely girl." And Spencer could see why. She *was* lovely. In every way.

She laughed. "Fine. I'll come." She squeezed his hand. "But only for your dad." The sun played tricks with her eyes, transforming them from brown to gold and back again.

The urge to kiss her was stronger than ever.

He had to stop this.

He let go of her hand and strode in front of her to the shed. "Let's go see the blossoms."

"Uh, Spencer?"

"Yeah?" He kept walking.

Distance.

He needed distance.

"Isn't the orchard that way?"

He didn't need to look to know she was pointing east, to where the cherry blossoms hovered like puffs of pink cloud above the earth. "Yep."

"So then why—?"

He pressed the keypad to open the shed's garage door and waited for the realization to dawn on her.

"Oh."

Behind the door sat the mud-caked ATV he hadn't had a chance to clean off. Spencer glanced over his shoulder, eyeing Sophie's clothes. She looked relaxed in a pair of jeans and a soft lilac shirt. In place of her usual heels, she wore a pair of running shoes. He grinned. Apparently, she'd learned from her first trip across his yard. He liked when she went casual like this.

No, make that loved it.

His gaze traveled to her eyes, which were comically wide.

"You up for this?"

Her throat bobbed as she swallowed, but she nodded.

"All right, then—hop on!" He swung a leg over the seat and watched as determination settled over her.

She strode to the machine, gave it one last apprehensive glance, and threw her leg over it behind him.

"That's my girl!" He caught himself. "I mean—"

But she was laughing, and she'd wrapped her arms around him, and he forgot whatever he'd been planning to say.

"You ready?" He managed to croak.

"Let's do this." Sophie's arms tightened around him as he throttled the ATV up slowly.

His heart on the other hand—that shot from zero to past all hope of recovery in half a second flat.

Spencer's fist overflowed with the petals he'd offered to carry for Sophie when her collection had become too large for her hands.

They'd left the ATV at the edge of the orchard and had been walking and talking for he didn't know how long.

Being out here, seeing the trees through her eyes, was refreshing. She exclaimed over every blossom-covered tree, stopped to examine a patch of grass or the occasional mushroom. At one point, she stopped to show him a spot where the petals had fallen to the ground in a near-perfect heart shape.

She listened as he explained the work they did to maintain the orchard through the seasons.

"Isn't it hard, though?" she asked now. "I mean, there are so many things you can't control."

He sighed and ran a hand over the top of his head. "Yeah, it's hard. And there are days I wonder if it's worth it. If we can keep the place afloat much longer. But then there are days like this . . ."

Perfect days.

She moved closer and nudged him with her shoulder. She felt it, too, didn't she? How right it was for them to be together. To be here.

His phone dinged with a text, and he stopped to fish it out of his pocket as Sophie kept walking, her face tipped toward the sky, hair dangling low down her back. It took an incredible force of will to take his eyes off her and check his phone.

The text was from Tyler. *ETA one hour.*

Spencer tucked the phone into his pocket. That meant they had to get back to the real world soon.

A gust of wind sent a torrent of blossoms dancing through the air. Ahead of him, Sophie began to twirl in the midst of them, her arms lifted to her sides. She spun faster and faster, until she collapsed to the ground in a heap of giggles.

Something in Spencer broke loose.

He didn't want to resist how he felt anymore. Was powerless to, anyway.

His footsteps were certain as he walked to her side and reached to help her up. "Come on, I want to show you something."

# Chapter 21

"Where are we going?" Sophie leaned into Spencer and yelled to make herself heard over the rumble of the ATV's engine. It was the tenth time she'd asked, and for the tenth time, Spencer shot her a mysterious look over his shoulder but didn't say anything.

"Hold on!" he yelled now.

"What?" She was already holding on. Never wanted to let go, if she was being honest.

"Hold—"

A spray of cold water sloshed over her. She let out an involuntary shriek and looked up in time to see they'd driven into a fast-flowing creek.

A wet, thick blob landed on her cheek, and she shrieked again. Water flowed into her shoes.

She tucked her head into Spencer's back, her arms instinctively tightening around his waist.

"Almost across," Spencer called, and a second later, she felt the front of the ATV lift, as if they were climbing a bank.

She waited a second to make sure she wasn't going to get wet again, then lifted her head. The bank was steep, but Spencer handled the ATV with a sure hand.

When they reached the top, he throttled down and brought the machine to a stop.

"Soph, I'm so sorry. I haven't been over here much this year, and I didn't realize—" But he broke off as he swiveled on the seat to face her.

His eyes widened, and his lips lifted a fraction as he fought to keep a straight face. And if she looked anything like he did, she didn't blame him. Mud speckled his hair, a glob stuck under his left eye, and his shirt had gone from white to brown more effectively than if it'd been dyed.

She felt her own lips lift into a smile. And then she was laughing.

A moment later, she was laughing so hard she was crying.

"What?" Spencer tried to deadpan but failed to hold back his own grin. "Did I get a little muddy?" He dabbed daintily at his face, and Sophie broke into another round of laughter. This time, he couldn't fight it. His deep laugh joined hers, and the sheer joy of sharing this moment made Sophie laugh even harder.

When their laughter finally subsided, Spencer became suddenly serious. "I am sorry I ruined your clothes, though."

Sophie glanced down. Both her jeans and her shirt were dotted with mud. But she didn't care. "They can be washed."

"And your face."

"You ruined my face?"

Spencer's eyes landed on hers, locked in place. "Nothing could ruin your face. It's perfect."

"Oh." She didn't mean to sigh at that, but how could she help it? Somehow, he always knew the right thing to say.

"But—" His gaze shifted to her cheek. "You do have a little something here." His fingers grazed her skin, brushed at her cheek.

She resisted the urge to close her eyes and lean into his hand.

She had sensed it growing all afternoon, this thing between them. But she had to be the strong one, the one who resisted the pull—for Spencer's sake.

"Should we—" Her voice came out too soft, and she tried again. "Should we keep going?"

Spencer swallowed. Nodded. Withdrew his hand slowly.

"So, where are we going?" She tried to channel some of the playfulness from before, but Spencer shook his head and throttled up the ATV.

For the rest of the ride, Sophie concentrated on making as little contact with him as possible without falling off the machine.

By the time he slowed the ATV, her shoulders were in knots from the effort.

"Here we are." Spencer waited for her to climb off, and she did, careful to grab his shoulder for only a second, just long enough to keep her balance.

"And where exactly is here?" Sophie spun in a slow circle, taking in the cornfield on one side, the edge of what appeared to be a small woodland on the other.

The sun had fallen low in the sky so that it just sparked on the treetops.

"It's beautiful," she breathed.

"It is." Spencer's eyes seemed to trace the edges of her face, and she turned away. If he looked at her like that one more time, she wouldn't be responsible for anything her lips may choose to do.

"But—" Spencer grabbed her hand and tugged her toward the trees. "This isn't what we're here for."

He pulled her into the stand of trees, and she let their earthy scent—the same scent she always associated with Spencer—wash over her. He led her on a weaving path through the trees, and she tightened her grip on his hand—only because her eyes hadn't adjusted to the low light in here yet. The dark must be the reason her blood thrummed in her ears, too.

Finally, Spencer drew to a stop. He turned toward her expectantly. She gazed around. All she saw was more trees.

"It's a forest." She didn't want to insult him, but if he wanted to show her trees, they could have saved themselves the walk.

"Close your eyes."

"What?"

He moved behind her and reached to cover her eyes. "Take ten steps forward." His breath tickled her ear.

"What?" She remained planted.

"Just trust me, Soph. Ten steps forward."

She wanted to remind him that she didn't do well with surprises, but she shuffled dutifully forward.

"Bigger steps." Amusement colored Spencer's voice. It sounded good on him.

"I don't want to crash and get hurt."

"I'd never let that happen." His voice—it was so soft, so sincere, she wanted to spin right there in his arms. One of his hands moved to her waist, and the other shifted to cover both eyes.

She widened her steps as he'd instructed.

"Seriously, Spencer, what is this about?"

But instead of answering, he nudged her a fraction forward. "Open your eyes."

⌇

Spencer didn't know why he should be so nervous. He wasn't the one who'd been walking with his eyes closed. Even if it felt like that's exactly what he was doing, bringing Sophie here, to this spot that held so much of his family's history. That he hoped might hold so much of its future.

He pulled his hand slowly away from Sophie's eyes, then shifted to stand next to her so he could watch her discover his favorite place on the whole farm.

He knew the moment she noticed the knotted old cherry tree in the center by the way her eyes widened. She moved toward it without saying anything. He walked next to her, feeling an odd sense of pride in the old tree and its blossom-rich branches.

"This is the tree the farm is named for. The hidden blossom tree. It's part of the original orchard planted by my great-great grandfather when he first settled here. The rest of the trees in this section were wiped out by disease long ago. But this one has stood through disease, storms, drought, you name it."

Up close, the fragrance of the tree's blossoms enveloped them.

"It's amazing." Sophie ran her fingers along a blossom-covered branch. On impulse, Spencer plucked a flower and tucked it behind her ear.

She lifted her hand to cover his.

He froze. Met her eyes. "You know, this spot is sort of part of a family tradition."

"Mmm?" The silk of her hair slid against his hand every time she moved a fraction.

"My great-grandparents got married in front of this tree, my grandpa proposed to my grandma here, and my parents had their first kiss under these branches."

"Wow," Sophie whispered, or maybe it was just a breath. He couldn't tell. Her eyes were too entrancing for him to think about anything else.

"Yeah, and—"

But he couldn't say anything else because Sophie's lips were suddenly pressed to his. Spencer's hand slid further into her hair as his lips responded. Her arms circled his neck, and she pulled him in closer.

Her lips were so familiar, and yet there was something new in her kiss, something he'd never felt before, something more open, more real, than anything between them had ever been before.

Somewhere in the back of his mind, a warning bell with a voice suspiciously like Tyler's sounded. Spencer tried to push it aside, but it was annoyingly persistent.

Gently, he moved his hands to Sophie's shoulders and pulled his head back.

At the look on her face—the combined contentment and confusion—he almost leaned in again.

But Tyler was right. He couldn't go through this again.

"I'm sorry," Sophie half-gasped. "I shouldn't—"

But he shook his head. "I'm glad you did." He couldn't deny that. "But we should get back." He pulled out his phone.

Sure enough, three new texts from Tyler:

*We're back.*

*Dinner's about ready. Where are you?*

*Starting without you. You better not be doing anything stupid right now.*

Spencer clicked off the phone. He wasn't doing anything stupid. Unless you counted kissing your ex-girlfriend as stupid. Your ex-girlfriend who was going back to Chicago. Your ex-girlfriend who was going back to Chicago, who you were still madly in love with.

Okay, maybe he was doing something a little stupid.

# Chapter 22

Sophie focused on keeping at least two feet of empty space between herself and Spencer as they walked through the trees toward the ATV. It meant she kept stumbling over roots and getting slapped in the face by branches she didn't notice until the last minute, but it was safer than getting too close to Spencer. Otherwise, she might give in to the temptation to kiss him again.

She couldn't quite bring herself to regret that kiss, even if it hadn't been fair to him.

She worked to take her thoughts off the soft brush of his lips against hers. They were so warm and—

She had to stop. "So do you think you'll stay on the farm your whole life? Or do you ever think about going back to school and finishing your degree?" She tried to ask it casually, to pretend there was nothing behind the question.

Spencer didn't slow his pace. "Yeah, I've thought about it. Especially after last year, when we almost lost everything. But Soph—" He stopped without warning, and she had to pull herself up short to keep from breaking her two-feet-of-space rule. "Sometimes it feels like this is what I was born to do. You know?"

Sophie nodded, even as her heart slid down through her feet and into the ground. He'd never consider the plan that had taken hold of her this afternoon. She'd thought maybe they could be together, maybe he'd be willing to move to Chicago with her, get his degree, get a job there.

But he was clearly more attached to this land than he was to her.

They walked the rest of the way to the ATV in silence. It wasn't until she was settling in behind him on the machine that he spoke again. "What about you? Do you think you'll be in Chicago forever? Or will you ever come home to Hope Springs?"

The question caught her so off guard that she opened her mouth to answer, then snapped it shut. She'd been so sure all her life that she'd never be willing to live here again. But—

"Right." In front of her, Spencer's back stiffened. The ATV roared to life, and Sophie had to make a mad grab for Spencer's shirt to keep from falling off backward as they took off.

She couldn't keep two feet between them on the cramped seat, but as they crossed the fields, she concentrated on making only as much contact as necessary to keep herself on the ATV. Which meant she got even wetter when they crossed the creek the second time.

By the time they parked in the shed, her teeth were chattering, and her legs were stiff. She swung gingerly off the machine, rubbing her hands up and down her arms.

All she wanted was a nice warm bath and a chance to snuggle under her blankets to wallow in thoughts of the man she couldn't have.

But she'd promised that man she'd have dinner with his family.

Spencer swung off the ATV, frowning at her. "You're drenched and cold. Let's get you inside."

He was soaked, too, but somehow he managed to pull off the mud-caked look. Just one more sign that he belonged here.

She should argue. Tell him she'd be fine. But she couldn't make her teeth stop chattering long enough.

As he led her inside, the warmth of the house embraced her. It wasn't only the temperature. It was the whole feel of the place. She'd noticed it the first time she was here and hadn't been able to stop thinking about it since. The house may not be fancy, and its decor might be lacking a certain sophistication. But this was a *home*. The word stuck in her head even as a violent shiver racked her frame.

"Here." Spencer slid past her and disappeared into a room down the hallway.

He emerged a few seconds later, holding out a sweatshirt. "You can change into this. The bathroom's down the hall, first door on the left."

Sophie eyed the sweatshirt. She should say no to wearing his clothes. It was too familiar. But the idea of being warm and dry was too tempting.

In the bathroom, she pulled off her sodden, mud-stained shirt and slipped the soft sweatshirt over her head. She pushed up the sleeves that reached well past her hands and pulled down the hem that hit her at mid-thigh.

The big UW loomed at her from the mirror, backward in its reflection, but Sophie recognized the shirt. It was the same one she'd worn countless times before. She'd claimed it from Spencer almost the moment they started dating, when she got cold at a football game, and he took it off to give it to her. She hadn't given it back until she'd packed up her apartment after graduation. Then she'd stuck it in a box with all his other stuff, except the plush giraffe she couldn't bear to part with, and mailed it to him here. She pictured him getting the box, opening it, finding the sweatshirt, and shame washed over her.

It was a miracle he'd even talked to her when they'd run into each other at the hospital, let alone stood by her through Nana's funeral and taken her to the orchard today. And returned her kiss.

The kiss that never should have happened, she reminded herself as she stepped out of the bathroom.

Spencer was setting a mug of coffee at the table when she walked into the kitchen. He stared at her in the sweatshirt as she settled onto the chair, a half-smile lifting his lips. "Remember when you spilled ketchup on that shirt?"

Sophie chortled. "How could I forget. I was afraid you'd break up with me. You were so mad."

Spencer held up a hand. "I wasn't mad, I was—" He shook his head. "Okay. I was mad. But only because I couldn't afford to buy another one, and I was afraid you'd leave me for some other guy who had a clean sweatshirt you could wear."

A laugh burst out of her just as she was about to take a sip of coffee. "I told you it would come out."

Spencer snorted. "That's only because we washed it like nine times. That's how it got so faded."

Sophie ran a hand down the faded letters. Truth was, she liked it this way. It made it feel familiar, like it had always been a part of her. A part of them.

She glanced up to find Spencer watching her. He cleared his throat. "I'd better go get changed so we can get to my parents' before there's no food left."

As he disappeared, Sophie wrapped her fingers around the mug, letting its warmth seep into her stiff knuckles. Her eyes fell on a stack of papers on the table, and she slid it closer. Maybe reading would keep her mind off Spencer.

But as she scanned the pages, her thoughts shifted to concern. If these pages told the farm's full financial story, it was in trouble.

Serious trouble.

Footsteps sounded in the hallway, and Sophie pushed the papers aside. She had no business going through Spencer's financial statements.

"Ready?" Spencer stopped in the kitchen doorway. He'd changed into a pair of dark jeans, and a blue button down that magnified the color of his eyes.

She pushed to her feet, stealing one last glimpse of the papers on the table to keep from staring at him.

Looked like the farm's finances weren't the only thing in trouble.

Her heart might be, too.

# Chapter 23

Spencer pressed his hand lightly to the small of Sophie's back, steering her out the front door of his house. Outside, the night's chill washed over him. Maybe that would clear his head of all the ridiculous thoughts swirling there. Force some common sense in.

All the way back on the ATV, the whole time he was making Sophie's coffee, all the while he'd been changing, he'd been turning over Sophie's question about staying on the farm forever.

He'd thought he sensed something under the question. Was she asking because she wanted to know if he'd leave the farm to be with her?

And if that's what she was asking, would he consider it?

It's not like living on the farm forever had been part of his original plan. He'd always intended to finish his degree and get a real job someday. But then he'd been here, and it'd been—not easy, but familiar. And he loved the land, loved its rhythms, loved working with his hands.

But he loved Sophie, too.

There was no point in trying to deny that anymore. At least not to himself.

So would he be willing to give this place up for her?

"Spencer?" Sophie's voice cut into his thoughts, and he realized she'd said something to him.

"I'm sorry. What was that?"

"I was just asking if your family will be upset we're late."

Spencer chuckled. If Mom knew he'd spent the afternoon with Sophie—which she probably did, thanks to Tyler—she'd be calling Pastor Zelner right about now to schedule the wedding. "They won't mind."

Except for Tyler. He'd sent another text while Spencer was making the coffee.

*Seriously, Spencer, not worth getting your heart broken again.*

But maybe he didn't have to get his heart broken. Maybe things could work out.

He could move to Chicago, or better yet, she could come back to Hope Springs.

*And be a farmer's wife?* The voice of reason cut through as his eyes fell on his parents' house, a fraction of the size of the home Sophie had grown up in. They walked down the short jog in the driveway that led to the tired-looking garage.

And anyway, hadn't her silence when he'd asked if she'd consider coming back said everything he needed to know?

She may have kissed him, but when it came down to it, she'd never pick him before her career or her accustomed lifestyle. It was why she'd said no to his proposal in the first place.

"Everything okay?" Sophie grazed his hand tentatively as they reached the front steps. "You're quiet."

He forced a smile she'd see through in a second. "Just thinking."

He opened the door, and a wall of sound from inside hit them. His smile became genuine as Dad's booming laugh carried to the door.

He couldn't worry about the future right now. He needed to take the time to celebrate this moment with his family.

He steered Sophie through the living room to the kitchen. Everyone was already at the table, one twin on Tyler's lap, the other on his mother's. Both boys were throwing more food than they were putting in their mouths. While Tyler was trying to make them stop, Dad's laugh boomed out again.

"Don't encourage them." But Tyler was smiling, too.

Oh, boy. What had he brought Sophie into? He was sure meals at her house never descended into chaos like this.

"I'm sorry, I—" But one glance at Sophie and his apology died on his lips.

Delight danced in her eyes, and her smile lit up her whole face. "This is wonderful," she whispered, leaning toward him.

He nodded, heart full. It was pretty wonderful. His family, all together in one place for the first time in years. And there was no one he'd rather experience this with.

He led her to the table and pulled out a chair. She gave him a look, but he just smiled and waited for her to sit, then kissed his mom on the cheek and clapped his dad on the back before taking the seat next to Sophie.

"You look good, Mr. Weston." Sophie took the bowls his mother started passing the moment they sat.

Spencer grinned as his father ducked his head and put on a gruff act. "Not back to full strength yet."

Spencer scooped some corn onto his plate. "Give it time, Dad. You'll get there." He leaned over to whisper to Sophie in a mock-conspiratorial tone, "Dad hates to sit still."

"Well, what's a man good for, if not to work?" Dad speared a piece of chicken. "I've felt worthless in that hospital room for the past week."

"You'll be back out there soon enough." Spencer pointed his fork at Dad. "Before harvest, for sure."

And once Dad was on his feet again, Spencer could start to think about his own life. About what he really wanted. Whether he could leave the farm for Sophie—assuming she wanted to be with him, of course.

"Actually." Mom set down her fork and gave Dad a significant look. "He won't be."

Spencer stopped with a forkful of chicken halfway to his mouth. "Well, maybe a little longer then, but—" He broke off at Mom's pointed stare.

His head swiveled to Dad, who was shredding a napkin.

"Your father," Mom began, but Dad interrupted.

"I'll tell them, Mary."

Now everyone's eyes swiveled to him. "But first I want to say something."

They all waited, everyone's forks still. A churning started in Spencer's gut. He felt like he had at the hospital—like he was waiting for bad news.

"I just wanted to say—" Dad's hands shoveled the shredded napkin pieces into a pile. "Thank you to all of you."

"There's nothing—" Spencer started to say, but his father held up a hand to stop him.

"No, I mean it. I know I haven't always been a perfect father, but I'm proud of the way I raised my sons. When I needed you, you both came through. Spencer—" When Dad's eyes lifted to him, Spencer felt the need to both sit up straighter and duck under the table. "You saved my life. And you've kept this farm running."

Spencer clenched his teeth together and blinked rapidly at the table with a short nod. Sophie's hand covered his, and she squeezed.

"And Tyler." Their father turned to Tyler, who held the twins on his lap—both now miraculously quiet as they munched on cookies. "I know we've had our rough patches. But when I needed you, you came home. And you brought me two of the greatest gifts I could imagine."

"You can keep them if you want," Tyler muttered, and they all laughed as Jonah shoved a mushy piece of cookie into his father's mouth. Tyler spluttered but grinned.

"And Sophie—"

Sophie's head shot up, and it was Spencer's turn to squeeze her hand. She looked utterly—and adorably—startled that Dad had singled her out.

"You brought me flowers. And you make my son happy. What more could I ask for?"

Spencer choked on his water. "Dad, we're not—"

Sophie laid a hand on his arm, and he stopped. "It's the least I could do."

Spencer studied her, but she pulled her hand away and refused to meet his eyes. Her cheeks had a slight glow to them.

"Alan," Spencer's mother said from next to him.

"Oh, yes, and my beautiful wife. Who hasn't left my side once in the past week and who has stood by me for thirty-five years." He grabbed her hand and brought it to his lips.

"You're welcome," Mom said, "but you know that's not what I meant." She gave him a stern look and twisted her hand to lace her fingers through his. Spencer had seen that look before. Something big was up.

His father stared at the table. "There's something else." He cleared his throat as they all waited. "This second heart attack has been kind of a wake-up call. Guess the first one didn't take." He plucked a piece of shredded napkin off the pile in front of him and set it off to the side. "But I want to be around to see my grandchildren grow up. Which means I need to take care of myself. Avoid stress." He blew out a long, slow breath. "That's why I've— We've—" He looked at Mom, who gave an encouraging nod. "We've decided to sell the farm."

Spencer dropped his fork but didn't bother to pick it up. "But you just said you feel worthless when you're not working."

Dad gave him a long, hard look, and Spencer struggled not to squirm under the scrutiny. He knew that look. It was the one Dad always gave when he was waiting for Spencer to catch on to something on his own. But he couldn't for the life of him figure out what it was.

"*Feel* worthless Spencer. Feel worthless. But I know I'm not worthless. I have worth to God—"

"And to us—" Mom piped up.

"And to my family," Dad agreed. "No matter what I do or don't do. No matter how I feel. So, I'm going to rely on that."

"Besides—" Tyler picked up a crying Jonah, who had banged his head on the table, and passed him to Dad. "Your job now is full-time grandpa." He glanced around the table. "We're going to stay in Hope Springs, if that's okay with everyone."

Next to Tyler, Mom burst into tears. "Ah, Mom." Tyler leaned over to give her a hug. He shot a look at Spencer, whose mind had gone completely blank. Dad was selling the farm. Which meant he wouldn't have to feel guilty if he left. But the thought of losing his family's legacy left him with a hollow feeling right in his middle.

"Sorry." Mom waved a hand in front of her eyes. "It's an answered prayer."

"Mary." Dad's voice held a note of warning. "We promised we wouldn't pressure them."

"I know. I know." She wiped at her eyes with a napkin. "Either way, I'm just glad I'll be near my grandbabies."

"Either way what? Pressure who?" Spencer was missing something. Mom sometimes forgot they weren't mind readers.

"I'd like to give you boys first option to buy the farm. Either alone or together. I'd give you a good price, of course, and we could work out fair terms. And . . ." He fell silent, and Spencer wondered if he was waiting for them to jump in. But he couldn't open his mouth, and even if he could, he wasn't sure what would come out.

Tyler looked equally dumbstruck. A fleeting moment of disappointment and maybe sadness flashed in Dad's eyes but then was gone. "Anyway." He stood and picked up his plate, but Mom plucked it out of his hands and pushed him gently back into the chair. Spencer didn't miss the concerned twist to her mouth.

"You don't have to decide right now," Dad continued. "Take some time to think about it. But please know this is your choice. I don't want either of you to feel obligated."

On his other side, Sophie shifted, and he made himself look at her, much as he dreaded seeing her reaction to his dad's offer. She was staring into her lap, where her fingers were twisting a purple ring.

Spencer turned back to Dad. He'd never hesitated to call this man his hero, so somehow he hadn't noticed until this very moment that he did look older, more fragile.

A fierce ache started in his gut at the thought that someday Dad wouldn't be around.

If selling the farm meant Dad would be with them longer, then that's what Dad should do. Even if it put Spencer into the position of deciding between his family and a future with Sophie.

Again.

"Yeah." He dragged a hand over his face. "I'm going to need some time to think about it."

# Chapter 24

"Thank you for dinner," Sophie said quietly to Spencer's family as she filed out the door Spencer held open for her.

His dad's announcement had put a damper on the celebration, and Spencer seemed in a hurry to leave. But once they were out the door, he shuffled toward his own house, barely seeming to notice Sophie was at his side.

The temperature had dropped enough that Sophie shivered and pulled her hands deeper into the sleeves of Spencer's sweatshirt.

Finally, she couldn't stand the silence any longer. "Are you going to buy it?"

Spencer pushed a hand through his hair and sighed so deeply she thought it would never end. "I don't know."

She gnawed her lip. She should keep her opinion to herself.

But the numbers on that financial statement haunted her. This place was barely staying afloat. One more bad year, and it would go under. She didn't want that for Spencer.

"Spencer." She reached for his arm, dragging him to a stop.

The tenderness in his eyes when he looked at her was its own kind of torture. What she was about to say might erase it for good.

But if she cared about him—and there was really no way she could pretend not to after their day together—she had to.

Cold air ripped at her lungs. "I saw the financial statements on your table."

He opened his mouth, but she jumped in. "I shouldn't have looked. I'm sorry. But—" She sucked in a sharp breath. "I have to tell you that in my professional opinion, it's not a good investment."

Spencer's eyes roved her face, and she wondered what he was searching for.

Instead of the anger she expected, he sounded defeated. "I know it's not. We were barely holding on, and then, after last year—" He tipped his head back and stared at the sky. There was only a sliver of moon tonight, and Sophie couldn't read his expression in the dark.

"But it's my home. My family's legacy." His Adam's apple bobbed. "I always imagined that one day I'd be picking cherries out here with my kids and then my grandkids. I just never really thought about owning the place. I guess I took it for granted that my dad would always be here."

Sophie nodded, even though his head was still tipped skyward and there was no way he could see her.

"Do you ever feel like a star?" His question came out of nowhere.

She wrinkled her nose. "Like a movie star?"

A gentle chuckle. "No." He pointed toward the sky. "A *star* star."

She leaned her head back, too. Thousands of stars created a tapestry of the night sky, and she drew in a stunned breath. When was the last time she'd let herself just look at the sky?

"How do you mean? Burning bright? Twinkling?" She tried to lighten the dark mood he'd fallen into. "You definitely sparkle, Spencer, if that's what you mean."

He offered a half-hearted smile. "I guess I was thinking about how many stars there are. How it seems to make each one insignificant."

Without thinking, Sophie closed the space between them and grabbed his arms. He pulled his gaze away from the sky, toward her. The doubt in his eyes—had that always been there, or was that her fault?

"You are not insignificant, Spencer. Didn't you hear your Dad in there? You saved his life. You've kept this place going. You matter. To your family. To God." It felt strange to be giving spiritual advice, given that she'd only just started thinking about God again herself, but she knew it was true. Spencer mattered to God. And so did she. The knowledge gave her courage to keep going. "And you matter to me, for the record."

For a moment, Spencer just watched her. Then he lowered his head toward her so slowly she thought time must have stopped.

When his lips finally met hers, the sigh that escaped her said everything she hadn't been able to put into words.

⌒⌒

Sophie woke up with a smile on her face. She could still taste Spencer's lips on hers. Still feel the gentle kiss he'd given her in the middle of Hidden Blossom's driveway and the one he'd given her when they reached her car—deeper, longer, more certain. It was a kiss that said she wasn't the only one with lingering feelings.

And with his dad's plan to sell the farm, Spencer was no longer tied here. He could leave—come to Chicago with her—without an ounce of guilt. It was perfect timing. Surely he had to see that, too. Otherwise, he wouldn't have asked her to dinner again tonight.

She felt light on her feet as she sped through getting dressed. She had plenty to do at Nana's before she could think about tonight. She'd better load up on coffee if she was going to get everything done.

But the argument that carried from the kitchen drew her up short in the hallway.

"I told you the bid was too low." Irritation snapped from Mom's voice.

Maybe Sophie didn't need coffee after all.

"It was a fair bid." Dad's retort was hard and firm. "If you want to make a profit, you can't go throwing money at people because you love the view."

"The view is what sells," Mom spat back.

The urge to flee, to run and climb under her blankets and cover her ears as she had when she was a child almost overpowered Sophie.

But she was an adult now. And a skilled negotiator to boot. She pulled her shoulders back and marched into the kitchen.

"Morning." She tried to keep her voice cheerful. "Everything okay in here?"

Mom and Dad were on opposite sides of the room—Dad seated at the table with a cup of coffee, Mom standing at the counter pressing buttons on the coffee maker. With a pang, Sophie remembered the way they used to huddle around their old coffee machine together, Dad sneaking a kiss the moment Mom turned to give him his mug. Mom swatting at him and telling him he'd burn himself, then setting the cup down to give him a deeper kiss. At the time, Sophie had been thoroughly disgusted. But now—now she realized what a rare thing they'd had. And they'd lost it. Just as she'd lost the rare thing she had with Spencer.

But maybe—

Maybe it wasn't too late.

"Everything's fine." Mom's sarcasm yanked Sophie back to the problem at hand. "If you consider losing possibly the best land on the peninsula as fine."

Dad rolled his eyes. "Don't be so dramatic, Katherine."

"Dramatic?" Mom plunked her coffee cup to the counter. "We could have put a whole villa on the Richardson estate. But your father wasn't willing to go high enough to get it. Now the Pearsons have it, and you know they're going to do something tacky with it. Probably another mini golf course."

"What's wrong with mini golf?" Sophie couldn't help the question.

Mom shot her a glare. "The point is, the market is prime for development, and we lost out on our best shot at it."

"They wanted too much for it." Dad's voice was the calm monotone that always infuriated Mom. "More land will come on the market soon enough."

"And when's soon enough, David? Six months? Nine? A year? Land like that doesn't ever just show up on the market anymore. Most of the big farms have already been pieced out, and the rest have no intention of selling."

"Actually, I might know someone who's selling." The words were out before Sophie could think about them. But as soon as she said it, it hit her—this was a solution that would benefit everyone.

Both of her parents swung their attention to her, and Sophie almost couldn't go on. She couldn't remember the last time she'd felt like the center of their world. What if they hated the idea?

But she had to put it out there. For Spencer's sake, if nothing else.

"I heard that Hidden Blossom Farms might go up for sale. I could probably convince the owner to entertain an exclusive offer."

"Is that the orchard in Silver Bay?" Her father sounded eager. "That's a prime spot. We've made numerous proposals to them, but they've never been interested in selling. Where'd you hear this?"

Sophie shifted in her seat. Was she doing the right thing, telling them? Spencer's father hadn't made his announcement in the hope of securing a buyer. But if she didn't step in, Spencer would let his sense of responsibility get in the way of the smart decision and anchor himself to a failing business. She couldn't let him do that.

There's no way he'd be able to match any price her parents could offer. The land was worth a million and a half, easy, and that would set him and his whole family up for a very long time.

"The owner has had some health problems," she said at last. "He's asked his sons if they want to buy it, but I don't see how they could . . ."

"We could get it for a pretty good price if they're desperate to sell." Her father pulled out his phone and started typing.

A twinge of conscience pinched at the edges of Sophie's heart. This wasn't what Spencer would want.

But she pushed the worry away.

Maybe it wasn't what he wanted.

But it was what he needed.

# Chapter 25

Spencer couldn't take his eyes off Sophie as he approached the spot where she stood at the end of the pier, gazing out over the water. A simple white sundress flowed around her legs, and her hair caught the light from the sunset.

He came up behind her and wrapped his arms around her shoulders, relishing the way she leaned into him, her light, flowery scent, the way her hands came up to rest on his arms.

These moments—the perfect kiss last night, the perfect dinner tonight, this perfect sunset—were only making his decision about the farm harder.

She shouldn't factor into his decision.

Rationally, he knew that.

But all day as he'd worked repairing fences and fixing equipment, he'd wavered back and forth. It seemed so unfair that choosing one thing he loved would mean giving up the other.

But he couldn't see any way around it.

Unless Sophie would be willing to stay here. With him.

Three times already tonight, he'd almost asked her. But every time, he'd chickened out.

He should ask her now, while they were standing wrapped together like this. But if he asked, he might shatter this moment. And it was too perfect to risk that.

Instead, he leaned toward her ear. "What are you thinking about?"

She shivered against him, and he wrapped her tighter.

"I was just thinking about that time we camped with Vi and Cade, do you remember?"

He nodded his head against hers, letting her hair caress his cheek. "I remember." His voice was soft with the memory.

Sophie had insisted she could never sleep in a tent, but she'd proved to be more outdoorsy than any of them had given her credit for. The two of them had sat up around the fire long after Violet and Cade had called it a night, talking softly about the past. And the future.

When they'd started yawning, they'd pulled their sleeping bags out of their tents and laid down next to each other to talk some more. As the fire's embers died, Spencer grabbed her hand, finally working up the courage to tell her the words that had been burning him from the inside out for weeks. "Sophie, I love you."

At first, she didn't move, didn't respond at all, and he thought she was trying to figure out how to let him down easy.

"I just wanted you to know," he added, kicking himself for not waiting to tell her. He knew it was too soon. That he had spooked her.

But then she rolled toward him, and in the firelight, he saw it in her eyes—she felt the same way. She wrapped her arms around him. And that was all he needed.

They stayed like that until she fell asleep. But Spencer laid awake for a long time, watching her. He had never been happier—or more terrified—than when he realized the depths of his feelings for her as she slept curled up next to him.

In the morning, he woke to find her watching him. "I do, too, you know." Her hair was mussed, and she had a groove in her cheek from sleeping on the ground all night, but she'd never looked more beautiful.

He pressed a kiss to her lips, his heart a mess of joy and hope and a knot of fear that he would never be able to give her the life she deserved.

"I'm never going to stop loving you," he'd promised in that moment.

She'd cocked her head to the side, as if trying to work out the meaning of the word *never*.

"Not until forever?" she'd asked.

"Not even then."

It was a promise he'd kept in spite of his best efforts not to over the past five years, he realized now. A promise he couldn't break if he tried.

"Soph." His voice barely worked.

"My parents still think I spent that weekend in Cancun with Vi." She laughed lightly.

She may as well have doused him with lake water. He loosened his grip around her shoulders and walked to the opposite edge of the pier.

Her parents.

She'd never told them about him. Obviously, she'd never been serious about him. About a future together.

"Spencer?" Sophie edged closer. "What's wrong?"

The lights of a small craft slid past the rocky breakwater, the soft chugging of its engine followed by the slap of its wake against the rocks.

He should forget it. Her family life was her family life, and he obviously would never be part of it. "Nothing. We should go."

"What? No." The desperation in her voice froze him. "Please tell me what it is."

He rounded on her. The last flickers of sunlight reflected off her eyes, and he had to look away. "Why didn't you ever tell your parents about me?"

"What?" Her brow wrinkled and her mouth dropped into a confused frown.

"My parents were ready to welcome you into our family when I proposed. And here you had never even mentioned me to yours. You introduced me to them as a classmate the other day. A *classmate*. Is that all I was to you?" He could feel the sneer twisting his lips. "Or are you too ashamed to tell them you dated a farmer? That he wanted to marry you?" He broke off, his breath coming in short gasps.

Sophie's sharp inhale told him he'd hit his mark.

Her hand fell on his arm, but he jerked away and stepped back. She wasn't going to get out of this with a soft touch.

Sophie lowered herself to sit on the pier, her legs dangling over the side, a foot or two above the water that had darkened to ink. Spencer peered into the bruised blue of the sky, trying to figure out how he'd let the night go so wrong. And yet, if this was going to work, she had to be real with him. They both had to be real.

She gestured for him to sit next to her. He watched the spot where her elegant fingers patted the rough boards. He should walk away right now. Protect his heart from any more damage.

But heaven help him, he couldn't bear to leave her looking so vulnerable and . . . unsure. Two words he never would have used to describe the Sophie he used to know.

He sat, kicking his own legs over the side of the pier.

When she was silent for a full five minutes, he finally looked at her. She was twisting the ring on her finger again.

"What is it?" He broke the silence.

She startled as if she'd forgotten he was there and followed the direction of his stare. "An amethyst. Nana gave it to me before . . ."

Three heartbeats of silence.

When she continued, her voice was stronger. "When she gave it to me, she told me that if I ever found love, I should hold on to it. But Spencer—"

She lifted her eyes to his, and he had to catch his breath.

"I was afraid. I *am* afraid." She tore her eyes away and squinted toward the horizon. "I'm not ashamed of you, Spencer." Her sigh floated on the wind. "I'm just—" She pressed her lips together.

Spencer waited, giving her room to gather her thoughts.

"My brother was planning to work with my parents, did you know that?"

Spencer shook his head but slid a fraction closer.

"Mom and Dad were so devastated to lose him that I just sort of tried to fill in for him, you know?"

Spencer lifted his head to watch her. She'd only been ten when her seventeen-year-old brother had died. That was a lot of pressure for a little girl to put on herself.

Her forehead wrinkled. "But my grades were never as good as his, and I was never an athlete, and I was terrible at music. I could tell my parents were disappointed with my efforts all the time."

"Oh, Soph." He slid the rest of the distance between them and wrapped an arm around her. How had she never told him this before?

"Is that why you went into real estate?" He gently turned her to face him.

The creases in her brow deepened. "I never really thought about it, but I guess so." She chewed her lip. "I confess I was hurt when they didn't offer me the job they were planning to give Jordan. Even though I probably wouldn't have taken it if they had. I wanted to show them what I could achieve on my own."

She shook her head. "Which doesn't answer your question about why I never told them about you. About us."

"You don't have to—"

She pressed a finger to his lips, and he couldn't have said anything more even if all the words he'd ever learned hadn't just flocked from his head in a mass exodus.

"I think." She turned the words over slowly. "I was worried that they wouldn't approve of you." Her fingers brushed back and forth over the worn wood of the pier. He tried to ignore the gut punch of her words. He'd been right after all.

But she grabbed his hand in both of hers, and he had to look at her. "I was afraid you wouldn't approve of them. Wouldn't like them." Her gaze dropped to her lap. "And then you would all stop approving of me. Would stop loving me."

His heart opened wide, and he wanted to wrap her in it. Had she really thought anything could make him stop loving her?

"Soph." He lifted her chin until she had no choice but to meet his eyes. "My love for you was never conditional. You never had to earn it." Her eyes closed, and he waited for them to open again. He needed her to know this next part. "You still don't."

He slid his arms around her neck and brought his lips to hers, letting the knowledge that he still loved her wash over them both.

In the distance, a boat's horn sounded a warning, but they ignored it.

# Chapter 26

Sophie sat upright in the passenger seat of Spencer's truck as he drove toward her parents' house. It was late—the clock on the dashboard showed well past midnight—but she was anything but sleepy. Every fiber of her being zinged with the awareness of Spencer's nearness. It scared her, her desire to be with him, but it also exhilarated her. His strong hand intertwined with her fingers.

She felt warm, protected.

Loved.

It was a feeling she'd missed. A feeling she'd longed for without realizing it.

She squeezed Spencer's hand, and he offered her that soft smile that made her stomach flip as if caught in a wave. He squeezed back.

For the fifth time, she opened her mouth to tell him she still loved him, too. But the same fear that had held her back the first time seemed to have clamped down on her vocal cords.

"Spencer?"

"Hmm." He lifted her hand to his lips and placed a gentle kiss onto her palm.

She closed her eyes. He was making this so easy for her. So why was it so hard?

"There's something I want to tell you."

He waited, and it took her three tries to swallow. She was going to say it this time.

But instead of the *I love you* she wanted to say, what came out was, "Why didn't you come after me?"

Spencer's head jerked toward her. "What?"

Sophie stared out the windshield. She could feel his gaze swiveling from her to the road and back again.

"That day. When you asked me to marry you. You didn't try to stop me when I left. You never called me. Never came after me." Her voice broke, but she pushed on. "Was I not worth it?"

She knew she wasn't being fair. His father had been sick. He'd had a lot to worry about. And she was the one who had walked away from him.

But still, she'd waited for his call begging her to reconsider. Telling her they didn't have to get married but that he still wanted to be with her. But it had never come.

The truck slowed, and Spencer pulled onto the shoulder, bringing it to a stop.

She shifted to look at him. "What are you doing?"

He slid the gear into park and flipped on the four-way flashers. "I need you to hear me when I say this." He angled in his seat so that he was facing her head-on. She felt the need to press toward him and draw back at the same time, but his eyes locked her in place.

He reached for her hand, and she let him take it. "You don't know how many times I almost called you, almost drove to see you. Not coming after you was the hardest thing I've ever done." His voice was ragged. "But when

I got home and looked around at what I had to offer you, I knew it wasn't enough. I knew you deserved more. So I let you go."

His hands slid up her arms, pulling her to him. "It was the biggest mistake I ever made." His voice was muffled by her hair.

Her arms went around him, too.

This was where she belonged.

With him.

Forever.

The word didn't scare her anymore.

She lifted her head and brought her lips to his.

Because she knew now.

Her home wasn't in Hope Springs. Or in Chicago. It was with Spencer. Wherever that took her.

⤬

Sophie paced the kitchen, running her fingers along the worn edges of Nana's journal. She'd read it cover to cover twice already, and the words were so precious to her that she couldn't wait to go through them a third time. But she knew someone else who needed them more right now.

She'd been waiting for Mom to appear for her morning cup of coffee for twenty minutes already. Maybe she'd missed her. If Mom was working on a big deal, she might have slipped out early.

Sophie couldn't wait to get on with her day. She'd been so busy cleaning at Nana's house yesterday that she'd only gotten to see Spencer for a few minutes when he stopped by to help her haul some of the bigger furniture to a local women's shelter. But they'd made plans for dinner tonight, and she and Vi were going to try to finish up the work at Nana's before then.

But she couldn't do any of that until she gave this to Mom.

Sophie eyed the counter. Maybe she should leave the journal there for Mom to find. It'd be easier anyway.

But no, there were things she had to say to Mom. Things she'd promised Spencer she'd say. Things she'd promised herself.

She poured herself another cup and set to pacing again. Finally, the click of Mom's heels announced her arrival. Sophie filled a second mug and passed it to Mom the moment she entered the room.

Mom eyed the outstretched mug, then took it from her hand, setting it on the counter to doctor it with the raspberry creamer Sophie had gotten out for her.

"Thanks," Mom finally said after she'd taken her first sip. "To what do I owe such service?"

If Mom noticed that Sophie's laugh was forced and nervous, she didn't let on.

"I just thought—" Sophie moved to the table. "I thought we could talk for a few minutes. Maybe?" She gestured toward the other chair, trying not to seem like a little girl seeking her mother's approval.

Mom's glance flicked to the clock on the stove. "I have about ten minutes before I absolutely have to leave. We're placing an offer this morning."

"That's great." Sophie waved a hand, barely listening. She had to clear her head for what she wanted to say.

Mom sat, sipping her coffee. Sophie stared at her mug, gathering her thoughts. Mom tapped her fingers on the table, and Sophie gritted her teeth.

Here went nothing.

"The thing is, Mom, I've realized lately how much of my life—how much of my energy—I've dedicated to trying to win your approval and Dad's."

Mom's mouth drew into the straight line Sophie had always associated with disapproval, and she quailed.

But she made herself push forward. "I think especially after Jordan—"

Mom sucked in a sharp breath and pushed to her feet.

Sophie slid her chair back and stood, too, blocking the exit. "I know you don't want to talk about Jordan. Or Nana."

Mom's face had gone whiter than the marble countertop.

"But at some point, you're going to have to face your feelings. Trust me, you can only keep them shoved into a corner of your heart and shut yourself off from the world for so long." She held out the journal to Mom. "When you're ready, I think this will help. Nana left it for me, but I think it's really a love letter to you, too."

Mom's lips trembled as she read the cover of the journal. Sophie stepped closer, until Mom had no choice but to take the journal or push Sophie backward.

She took it in a shaky hand.

"And if you ever wanted to talk—about anything—I'm here." Sophie's whisper cut through her ache for Mom to wrap her in her arms.

But Mom didn't move.

Sophie took a step back, blowing out a long breath. She'd said what she'd come to say.

But when she reached the hallway, she realized there was something else she wanted Mom to know.

"I love you, Mom."

Mom's silence followed her down the hall and out the door.

# Chapter 27

The diamond was smaller than he remembered, but it still sparkled.

Spencer's hand trembled slightly as he held the tiny box out in front of him, toward the mirror. The ring had been buried in the bottom of his sock drawer for five years. Could he really present it to her again? Risk her rejection again?

But after the last few days, he knew. She was the woman he was meant to be with, and he wasn't going to let his fear—or hers—stop him. He would just have to make her see how much he loved her. How he would spend the rest of his life doing anything for her.

Even if it meant leaving the farm he loved.

If that's what she wanted, he'd give it up in a heartbeat. The farm wasn't his life.

She was.

"Hey, Spence—"

Spencer snapped the case shut and whirled away from the mirror at the sound of his brother's voice. But based on the open-mouthed stare Tyler speared him with, he'd been too slow.

"So." Tyler pushed into the room uninvited and plopped onto Spencer's bed.

"Come in," Spencer muttered, shoving the ring box back into his drawer. But when he turned to confront Tyler's hard glare, he wished he still had something to occupy his hands.

"What?" He didn't mean to snap, but he hated the mix of pity and understanding Tyler was directing at him.

"You're not really going to go down that road again, are you?"

"What road?"

Tyler pointed toward the dresser, and Spencer could swear he was using X-ray vision to see right through the wood to the spot where he'd nestled the ring.

Spencer planted his feet in a defensive stance. "I was thinking about it."

Tyler stood and walked toward the door, then wheeled around and strode toward Spencer. He clapped a brotherly hand on Spencer's shoulder. "Spencer, do you really want to put yourself through that again? Emma told me how hard it was for you to get over that woman the first time and—"

"Her name is Sophie." Spencer's fingers clenched into a fist, and his shoulders tensed.

"Easy." Tyler held up his hands. "I know her name. And I like her, I really do. She's good with the twins. And she's nice and funny."

"Then what's the problem?"

"But that doesn't mean she's worth risking your heart for again. Just because everything seems perfect right now doesn't mean it's going to stay that way. And what about the farm? We should at least talk about that before you get carried away and do something irrational."

But it wasn't irrational. It felt like the most rational thing he'd done in months, years maybe—following his heart instead of his duty.

"Let me ask you something." Spencer pinned Tyler with his stare. They hadn't talked much about Julia since Tyler came back. Spencer had wanted to give his brother the space he needed to deal with everything.

But now, he needed to know.

"Let's say Julia showed up here tomorrow. Or next week. Or three years from now. And she told you she was sorry. That she still loved you. Could you really walk away from that second chance?"

Tyler opened his mouth, then slammed it shut and stalked out of the room.

"That's what I thought," Spencer called after him.

⸎

Sophie laid another Christmas decoration from her grandmother's collection into the box of items she wanted to keep. The basement was almost empty, and then she'd be done cleaning out the house. She'd have no more excuses to stay in Hope Springs—except her own desire.

"That nutcracker is too cute." Vi bounced down the steps after a trip upstairs with a box full of items she was going to sell in her store.

Sophie held it out to her. "Better start another box for the store."

"You don't want it?" Vi pushed her wild curls out of her face and snapped a ponytail around them.

"Are you kidding? These things kind of creep me out." She gave an exaggerated shudder. "Anyway, I already have way more stuff than I can fit in my apartment."

Unless she didn't go back to her apartment. If she stayed . . .

"Hey, Soph, can I ask you something?" Violet's voice was quiet, serious, as if she'd sensed the direction of Sophie's thoughts.

Sophie waited, even though she already knew the question.

"What are you doing? With Spencer, I mean."

Sophie grabbed a snow globe off the shelf and examined it. Inside, two figures stood with their arms around each other in the yard of a cozy-looking house. "Honestly? I don't know."

Vi passed her a sheet of newspaper to wrap the snow globe. "I think you need to figure it out. Before you get his hopes up. He doesn't deserve to be hurt again."

Sophie blinked back a sudden wave of emotion. Didn't her friend realize she already knew that? Spencer deserved only good things. Only everything. "The last thing I want is to hurt him."

"I know." Vi plucked a glass ornament off the farthest reaches of the shelving unit. "But if you let him think there's something there, that you—"

"I still love him, Vi."

Vi fumbled the ornament. She caught it just before it smashed to the floor.

"You do?" Vi's smile was genuine, but Sophie felt a pang for her friend. Vi had never doubted her love for Cade, would never have chosen to let him go, but she hadn't been given a choice in the matter.

"I mean—" Vi set the ornament gingerly into the box. "I knew that, but I was afraid you wouldn't realize it until it was too late."

Sophie could only grin at her friend, who'd always been better at reading her than Sophie was at reading herself.

"So does that mean you're staying? You're not going back to Chicago?"

Sophie lifted her arms helplessly. She had no idea what it meant. Only that she was open to the possibility. "Maybe?"

Vi squealed and dove at her for a hug. "I'll take maybe."

Sophie returned the hug, but a new bout of questions assailed her.

"Uh oh." Violet pulled back. "I know that look."

"What look?"

"The one that says you're not sure you're making the right decision."

Sophie gnawed at her bottom lip. "Well, am I? I mean, am I crazy to consider giving up a job a lot of people would kill for, a life in the city I've always dreamed of living in, to come back to the one place I've always wanted to escape? I mean, what if Spencer doesn't want— What if he doesn't feel—?"

Vi laughed gently. "If you can't see how Spencer feels, you're denser than I thought."

"Yeah, but—" Sophie ignored her friend's teasing tone. "I don't deserve a second chance. Not after how I left things last time." She passed a hand over her eyes. "I don't really deserve a second chance with you, either, come to think of it."

Vi shook her head. "You know, Soph, for a smart woman, you sure are slow sometimes."

"Hey." But Sophie waited for her to go on.

"You've always worked so hard to prove yourself, to earn everything, to be the best. But some things you don't have to earn. They're just . . . gifts."

"But—"

Vi raised a hand to silence her. "That's the thing, there are no buts. I forgive you and so does Spencer."

Sophie looked away and wiped at her eyes. What had she done to deserve such amazing people in her life? According to Vi, nothing, apparently. They were a gift. One she treasured.

Vi's arms wrapped her in another hug. "As far as staying, I can't tell you if it's the right move or if it's crazy." She let Sophie go and wrapped another ornament in tissue paper. "Have you prayed about it?"

Sophie stared at her friend. How did she always know what to do? Of course she should pray. Had it really been so long since prayer—since God—had been a regular part of her life that she never thought of it anymore?

"I will," she promised. She grabbed the tape gun and ran it across the last box. "There. Now I have four days free. What should we do?"

Vi ogled her. "*You* should get yourself over to Spencer's and tell him how you feel."

"Oh, but—" In theory, yes, it was what she was dying to do. But now that she faced the possibility of actually doing it—impossible.

Her phone blared, making them both jump.

Sophie set down the box she'd been about to haul upstairs. Her heart accelerated. She had no idea what to say to Spencer, and she didn't want to do it over the phone.

"Tell him," Vi chanted as she grabbed Sophie's abandoned box and started up the stairs.

Sophie tried to take a calming breath, but it was only halfway in when her eyes fell on the name on her screen.

Chase.

She deflated. She should let it go to voice mail. But she'd ignored every single one of his calls since she'd sent him back to Chicago. It was time to face up to him.

"It's a good thing you decided to answer this time." Chase's voice was hard-edged.

Sophie's stomach clenched. She hadn't exactly expected a warm greeting, but his anger threw her.

"I'm sorry, Chase. I've been busy here and—"

"I don't need your apologies. I just called to tell you that you need to be back here tomorrow morning."

"Tomorrow? But—"

"Or don't bother to come back at all."

"What?" Sophie tried to figure out exactly what he was saying. Was he threatening her? "If this is about—"

"It's not about anything, Sophie." Chase's voice softened. "I got the VP position, and my first job as VP is to call to inform you that company policy states that vacations of more than three days must be approved a month in advance, and since yours wasn't—"

Heat flooded Sophie's chest. "If you think burying my grandmother was—"

"As we understand it, the funeral was last week. The extra time off this week is a vacation. And your vacation is done." He hesitated a beat. "So will I see you tomorrow at eight, or should I have Tina pack up your office?"

Sophie pinched the bridge of her nose. This wasn't really happening. Sure, she'd been considering leaving Chicago, but it wasn't a decision she could make this moment, this way. She needed to think it through. Talk to Spencer. Figure out what she really wanted.

"Sophie?" Chase's voice held a trace of impatience.

"I don't— I don't know." She hung up before he could remind her what she'd be giving up if she didn't return.

Her hand shook as she dropped the phone to the makeshift workbench Nana had fashioned out of sawhorses and an old countertop. She braced herself against the counter, but it shifted and toppled to the ground with a crash.

"Everything okay down there?" Vi's voice was followed by her hurried footsteps on the stairs.

"Yeah." Sophie kicked at a disfigured sawhorse as she picked up her shattered phone. "No."

Vi moved closer, concern in the lines around her mouth. "Did Spencer not—?"

"It wasn't Spencer. It was my boss. He said I have to be back by tomorrow or I'm out a job."

"What?" Vi's hands slammed to her hips. "He can't do that. He—"

"Actually, he can." She'd been so excited to get this job that she'd read through the company handbook four times before her first day. Chase was right about the vacation policy.

"Okay, then. Why don't you quit? You said you were thinking about staying anyway, and—"

"*Thinking* about. Not going to do it this very minute." Sophie rubbed at her temples. Why did everything have to get more complicated the minute she thought she had things figured out? "I have a lot to consider. I haven't even talked to Spencer yet, and—"

"So go talk to him." Vi grabbed her arm and dragged her up the basement steps toward the front door.

"I don't have time. If I'm going to be back in the office by tomorrow morning, I have to take off right now."

"Make time." Vi's voice was firm.

"I can call him when I get to Chicago." She glanced at the splintered screen in her hand. "Once I get a new phone."

The thought left a hole in Sophie's heart, but what else was she supposed to do? "I can always come back. It's not like I'll be stuck there forever."

"Sophie Olsen." Vi's dark eyes flashed. "We both know if you run back to Chicago, you won't come home. And sure, you'll save your job. But you might lose everything that really matters."

"I'm sorry, Vi. This isn't how I wanted to leave." She leaned in and gave Vi a quick hug, then pushed out the door and jumped into her car before she could see the look of betrayal she was sure Vi wore.

# Chapter 28

Spencer lifted his shirt to wipe at the sweat dripping from his face. He jogged across the yard toward the house. He should have just enough time to shower before Sophie arrived. It'd taken all afternoon, but everything was finally ready. Using the ATV to haul the bench from his workshop to the hidden blossom tree had been a bear, but it was totally worth it. It was the perfect spot to do this—to carry on the family tradition.

He'd pack a picnic, they'd take the ATV to the clearing, enjoy dinner together. And then, on the bench he'd made for her, he'd tell her he wanted forever with her.

"Hey, Spencer." Dad's voice from behind caught him as he was about to open the door.

He turned. Dad was looking so much better it was amazing. Probably thanks in large part to the fact that Mom wouldn't let them say a word to him about how things were going on the farm or about their decision. Not that they'd made one yet.

But Spencer hoped to know more after tonight. If Sophie said yes to him—*please, Lord, let her say yes*—they'd make the decision together. And he'd be willing to do whatever she was comfortable with.

"What's with you?" Dad reached the steps and thrust a plastic dish into his hands. "Here, your mother sent this."

Spencer took the dish, barely glancing at the cookies inside.

"Nothing's with me. What are you doing here?"

His father pushed past him into the house. "I came to talk to you about the farm."

"Yeah, Dad, I haven't made my decision yet. I might know more after tonight, but . . ." Spencer pushed a hand through his hair.

"Well, that's what I came to tell you." His father grabbed the container back out of Spencer's hand and snatched a cookie. "Don't tell your mother." He took a bite of the cookie and closed his eyes. "Oh, that's good."

Spencer checked the time. Sophie would be here in ten minutes. "Look, Dad, can we talk about this another time? I kind of have plans."

Dad sniffed at the air, then moved into the kitchen, like a dog following a scent trail. "Is that fried chicken I smell?"

"Yeah." Spencer followed his father, trying not to let his exasperation show. "Sophie's coming over, so . . ."

"That's great. Maybe I'll hang out. I haven't seen her in a while. She brought me flowers, you know."

Spencer's mouth worked. Having Dad here when Sophie arrived was not part of the plan. "Dad—"

His father laughed and winked. "I'm leaving already." He slugged Spencer on the shoulder. "I just wanted you to know that if you decide not to buy, we'll be okay. We got an offer today."

Spencer blinked at his father. "An offer? I thought you were going to wait to put it on the market until Tyler and I decided."

His father held up a hand. "Before you go getting all offended, I didn't put it on the market. I don't even know how they heard about it. But it's a good offer. Really good."

"How good?" Spencer's eyes narrowed. Was this Dad's way of telling him he'd rather sell outside the family?

"It's good. I'm not going to name numbers right now because I don't want you to feel pressured to meet it if you do decide to buy. But just know that you shouldn't feel obligated to buy just to help me out."

"Who's the offer from?"

His father shrugged. "A development firm. Olsen, I think. They want to develop it into a resort or something. Condos, maybe. I don't remember the exact details."

But Spencer had stopped listening. "Olsen?"

Dad nodded, snatching another cookie. "I'll go so you can get ready for your date." At the door, he turned. "Tyler mentioned that you were planning to ask a certain question tonight. Think he wanted me to stop you. But sometimes you have to let go of the past to have the future you dream of." His sigh was deep. "Just like me and this farm."

But Spencer couldn't think about the past or the future right now. All he could think about was Sophie. He'd been willing to give up everything for her. Only it turned out she'd already made that decision for him. All to make her parents a few bucks.

# Chapter 29

Sophie couldn't stop the bouncing of her leg against the car's seat, the drumming of her fingers on the wheel, the slamming of her heart against her rib cage.

It'd taken her all of ten minutes to pack up her stuff at her parents' house. A mix of relief and regret swirled in her gut at the fact that neither had been home. She'd left a note, promising to come back soon. A promise she already doubted she'd keep. Not that her parents would care.

Vi's words hadn't stopped playing through her head since she'd left Nana's. *We both know if you run back to Chicago, you won't come home.* She wanted to deny it, but the past two weeks had felt so much like a dream. Maybe it was best if she kept it that way. Dreams couldn't disappoint the way real life could.

Sophie slowed as she drove through the downtown. A young couple stood arm-in-arm on the pier, two children pressed against their legs. She had to look away to keep the wave of longing from overtaking her.

The clock on the dashboard caught her eye. She was supposed to have been at Spencer's fifteen minutes ago. She hated the thought of him standing there, waiting for her.

Realizing she'd run away from him again.

*No.*

She couldn't do that to him.

Not this time.

She pressed her foot to the brake, drawing a sharp honk from the car behind her. She lifted a hand in apology, then took a hard left.

Vi was right. She had to talk to Spencer. See where his head was. Where his heart was. If he wanted her to stay, well, then she wouldn't have to worry about whether she had a job to go back to.

And if he didn't—she could drive all night to get back by morning if she needed to.

The thought that he might not want her to stay—that he might tell her to hurry back to Chicago because she was too late here—was almost enough to make her drive right past his house. But she was done running from her feelings. She'd see this through, no matter what that meant for her heart—no matter what kinds of feelings she'd have to deal with as a result.

By the time she pulled into the now-familiar driveway of Hidden Blossom, she felt calmer, more at ease, than she had in months.

She didn't know what she was going to say or how Spencer would respond, but she could almost picture his huge smile, the way he'd wrap his arms around her and kiss her in that slow, sweet way he did. The way he'd ask her to stay.

The second the engine stopped, she sprang out of the car. In her tennis shoes, it was an easy jog across the lawn. The clean air buoyed her as she knocked.

A moment later, the door pulled open.

She squinted against the sun that hovered just above the edge of the house's roofline. She made out his dark shirt and jeans first. "Sorry I'm late. Something came up and—"

Her words died as her gaze fell on his face. His jaw was set, his eyes hard. He pushed out the door. She took a step to the side as his presence filled the whole porch. The loathing in his expression was more than she could bear, and she shifted her gaze to the edge of the porch, where newly opened azaleas bobbed in the gentle breeze.

"Hey." She tried to keep her voice light, but his glare made it hard.

"You told your parents the farm was for sale." It wasn't a question.

Her eyes jumped to his in surprise. "Yeah. Did they make an offer?" Good thing she hadn't quit yet. Maybe he wanted to move to Chicago.

"Why would you do that?" He sounded like a hurt little boy, and Sophie moved closer, but he stepped back.

She pursed her lips. Couldn't he see she'd done him a favor? "I thought it would make things easier for you. I know you have this inflated sense of duty, and I respect you for that. But I didn't want to see you strap yourself to a place that was about to fail."

Spencer folded his arms across his chest, a barrier between them. "You didn't do it for me, Soph." His voice was quiet but sharp. "You did it for you."

Sophie shook her head. How could he not understand this was for him?

"No point in denying it. You've made it clear plenty of times that your parents' approval means more to you than anything else. Than me." He thrust the words at her like knife jabs, and she wanted to hold out a hand like a shield, but he kept going. "You never thought the life of a farmer was good enough. Never thought I was good enough."

Sophie reared back. Is that what he really thought of her?

Her mind went blank. She opened and closed her mouth, then turned away. It had been a mistake to come. One she'd regret for the rest of her life.

"You want to know the ironic thing, Soph?" Spencer gave a sharp, humorless chuckle. "I was going to ask you what you wanted me to do with the farm. I was going to offer to give it up for you. If that's what you wanted. All I wanted was a life with you. But you've made it clear how you feel about a life with me. So I guess I'm free to make this decision for myself."

Sophie bit the inside of her cheeks, hard. She should tell him he was wrong. That she'd done it because she loved him. But what if he was right? What if she'd told her parents about the farm for her own selfish reasons?

She ignored the sting at the back of her throat. "I'm sorry, Spencer. For everything. I actually just came by to tell you that I have to get back to Chicago. My boss expects me in the morning. So I'm going to have to cancel our dinner."

Spencer froze, his eyes locked on her face. She waited, her breath caught in her throat. Even after everything he'd said, some small part of her still hoped he'd ask her to stay.

But when he looked away, she knew.

She stepped to the lawn. "Bye, Spencer."

Somehow, she managed to keep the tears at bay until his farm was out of sight.

Everything in Spencer told him to go after her.

Everything.

But he resisted. She had betrayed him. She had no interest in a life with him. And she'd been planning to leave all along.

He ripped the door open and barreled into the house.

Inside, the smell of the fried chicken taunted him. He pulled it off the counter and dumped it into the trash.

When he sat, something pressed against his thigh.

He shoved his hand into his pocket and ripped out the ring box. He moved to throw it into the trash, too.

But at the last minute, he pulled his hand back.

Instead, he opened the junk drawer and tossed it in there.

That's what his proposal would have been to her, anyway.

# Chapter 30

Sophie lifted the hair off the back of her neck, seeking any hint of a cooling breeze. The Chicago summer had been unbearably hot, and the concrete jungle offered little shade. She longed to throw on a pair of shorts and a t-shirt and lounge along the lake, but that wasn't going to happen.

In the two months since she'd returned, she'd been pulling twice her weight, trying to reestablish her loyalty. Earn a shot at the next promotion, since she'd blown the last one. That's what happened when you let your heart get in the way.

The only bright spots in her weeks had been Sunday mornings. She'd found a charming little church where she could let go of all the cares of the world for an hour and just focus on worshipping. Last Sunday, after church, she'd found herself confiding to the white-haired pastor that she felt lost. He'd given her the same encouragement Vi had months ago—pray. Only this time, she had listened. She'd spent hours that afternoon walking along the lake. *I don't know your plans, Lord, and it scares me to give over control of my life, my future. Help me to trust you to lead me to the life you know is right for me.*

The words of Nana's journal still burned in her heart, and she'd prayed about that, too—about finding her worth in God and nowhere else.

The words still had a grip on her as she forced herself to put one foot in front of the other now. All week, it had gotten harder and harder to go to work. Everything she saw, everything she did, seemed to be nudging her toward where she really wanted to be.

Like the leaves that hung limp and listless in the humid air. They made her think of the rows and rows of trees in Spencer's orchard rustling in the cool lake breeze, raining cherry petals around her. When had she been happier?

She pushed through the doors of the office building, shivering in the sudden artificial cold of the air conditioning. As she squeezed onto the nearly full elevator, she pushed down a surge of panic at being in the confined space with so many people. She tried to direct her thoughts to something more pleasant. But they fell on their default: the memories of Spencer that lingered like a kiss.

*Stop it. Thinking about Spencer isn't going to help you move on.*

Sophie focused on taking deep breaths until the elevator stopped on her floor. By the time she stepped out, she was calm. Focused. Ready to get to work.

Chase accosted her the moment she stepped through the office doors. He pushed a coffee into her hands, along with a folder bulging with papers.

"There's a snag in the Hudson project. I need you on it right away. We can't lose this one."

Sophie took a swig of the coffee, yanking the mug from her mouth as the hot liquid scalded her tongue. She ignored the burn and opened the folder. But the renderings blurred in front of her. The folder seemed to weigh her down, root her to the spot.

A sudden certainty slammed into her. She didn't want this life. She'd made it her dream because she'd thought it was what would make her parents proud, earn their approval. But if she was honest with herself, this had never made her happy.

"I'm done." She said it so softly she wasn't sure anyone had heard. "I'm done." She said it louder this time. Like she meant it.

Chase gave her a bemused smile. "What do you mean, you're done? We've got a few more things to do on this one before we can call it finished."

"No. I mean I'm done. With this. All of it. I quit."

She set her coffee cup on the nearest desk and spun on her heel. She was at the office door before she realized the enormity of what she was doing. But it was the right thing.

Chase grabbed her elbow as she was about to hit the elevator button. "Don't do this, Sophie." She let him lead her to the large bank of windows that overlooked the bustling sidewalk. The crammed street. "You're upset about something. I can see that. But don't ruin your career over it."

Sophie offered a soft smile. She and Chase had worked past the initial awkwardness after her return, and she now considered him not quite a friend—but the closest thing she had to one in the city. She appreciated his concern.

"I'm not upset. I just realized that this"—she gestured around the luxurious office—"it's not right for me."

"That's fine. I get it. But if you walk out like this, you're never going to find a position with another firm. Stay on until you get another job. I'll write you a recommendation."

Sophie shook her head. "You don't understand. I don't want another job. This isn't what I was made to do. I only did it because—" She paused. How did she explain? "Well, it's a long story, but let's just say I'm not passionate about it the way you are."

Chase wrinkled his nose. "So what will you do?"

Sophie bit her lip. The truth was, she wasn't sure. But for some reason that didn't bother her. "Go home for a while. See if there might be something for me there." *Or someone.*

Chase studied her for another minute, as if unsure what to make of her. Then he leaned over and gave her a quick, semi-awkward hug. "Take care of yourself."

Sophie stepped onto the elevator and offered a small wave.

She may not know what she wanted to do with her life.

But she knew who she wanted to share it with.

If it wasn't too late.

# Chapter 31

Spencer jiggled little Jeremiah on his lap as he signed his name for the twentieth time.

"Just a few more papers," their banker said. Spencer groaned. He'd also said that forty-five minutes ago. But he was grateful the man had been willing to come out to the house to do the closing paperwork. He couldn't imagine trying to corral these two energy balls in a bank.

He passed the paper to Tyler so his brother could add his signature.

"You're sure about this?" Spencer studied Tyler for any signs of a change of heart.

Tyler snatched the paper out of Jonah's grabbing hand and gave him a clean sheet and a crayon instead. "Would you stop asking me that? I said I was sure."

"Sorry." Spencer tapped his pen against the table. "It's just that you used to be so dead set against this place. I want to make sure you're not doing this out of some sense of obligation or something."

"Have you ever known me to do anything out of a sense of obligation?" Tyler signed his name next to Spencer's on the closing documents. "That's your territory."

Spencer grunted as he signed his name again. But the truth was, he wasn't doing this out of any "inflated sense of duty" as Sophie had accused him. He really did love this land and the legacy it represented. He wanted it to be here to pass on to his children someday. Assuming his heart ever recovered enough from Sophie to meet someone else and start a family. But even if he didn't, at least it would go to his nephews.

"Anyway." Tyler grabbed the next form to sign. "This place has a way of growing on a person."

"Some people, maybe," Spencer muttered.

His brother was watching him, but Spencer concentrated on scanning the forms in front of him.

"Are you just going to make all these veiled references to Sophie for the rest of our lives without ever actually talking about her?"

Spencer shrugged. It seemed to be working for him so far.

"You should call her." Tyler slid another form back to the banker.

Spencer snorted. "Says the guy who told me not to propose again. Learn to quit when you're ahead."

"Yeah, about that." Tyler scrubbed a hand across his buzzed hair. "I may have been wrong. I was projecting my own feelings about Julia onto your situation. And anyway, you were right. If I had another chance, I'd take it." Tyler nudged Spencer's phone closer to him. "Just call. It's clear you're miserable without her."

"I'm not miserable." He scratched his signature across yet another form. Would they never be done with this blasted paperwork? He had other things to do. Namely, escape his brother's interrogation.

Tyler let out a disbelieving *humph*. "Boys, is your uncle Spencer happy?"

Both boys looked at him. Ridiculous. Now he was being psychoanalyzed by three year olds?

Jonah shook his head, his expression somber. "Aunt Sophie gone."

Jeremiah nodded his agreement. "When coming back?"

Tyler cleared his throat. His grip on the pen in his hand tightened. Spencer understood. It was the same question the twins had asked about their mother every day for the first month and a half they'd been here.

The banker coughed lightly. "Last one." As soon as they'd signed, he held out a hand to shake each of theirs. "Congratulations." In spite of their argument, Spencer grinned at Tyler. They were really doing this. Together.

Spencer ushered the banker to the front door, thanking him again for making the process relatively painless. If only he had a series of papers Spencer could sign to guarantee he'd get over Sophie.

He'd been working at it all summer. But with no success. Every time he closed his eyes, he saw her expression when she'd turned away from him that last time. She'd looked so . . . broken. That was the only word for it.

Only days before that, he'd promised his love for her was unconditional. But the moment she'd done something he didn't like—didn't approve of—he'd sent her away. What kind of example of Christ-like love was that?

"Hey, you got any tape?" Tyler called from the kitchen. "Jonah wants to wrap up his picture for grandma and grandpa."

"Yeah, check the junk drawer." Spencer gave the land—their land—one last look before closing the door. If anyone had told him ten years ago he'd be buying the farm with his brother—not to mention living with him—he'd have laughed in their face. He'd all but written Tyler off when he left. But it had only taken two months for his brother and nephews to find a place in his life. Even if his house sometimes felt overcrowded and not so much his own anymore. He couldn't imagine things any other way.

"Ah, Spencer?" Tyler's voice carried to him as he made his way to join them in the kitchen.

"Yeah?" But he froze in the kitchen doorway.

Tyler held a little black box. He'd opened it and was staring at the ring inside.

Spencer snatched the box out of Tyler's hand, opened the cupboard under the sink, and chucked the box in the trash can there.

But Tyler pushed past him and grabbed it out. He held the box toward Spencer, but Spencer refused to take it.

"Look, Spencer." Tyler closed his hand around the ring box. "Maybe it's time to put your pride aside. You clearly still love her. And if you wait, eventually it will be too late."

"It's already too late." Spencer spat the words at his brother. Why couldn't Tyler learn when to butt out? "I've just committed myself to this farm. You think that's the kind of life she can accept?"

"I think—" Tyler set the ring box on the counter. "I think if she's the woman you've made her out to be, then none of this"—he gestured at their surroundings—"will matter to her. I think you've convinced yourself you can't give her the life you think she wants because it means you don't have to put yourself out there. But what if her lifestyle isn't what she cares about? What if all she cares about is you?"

Spencer stared at the box.

Tyler meant well.

But he was wrong about what Sophie wanted.

Wasn't he?

"Hello?" The gruff male voice on the other end of the phone sounded irritated.

And no wonder. This was the third time in a row Spencer had called. He couldn't make himself believe that Sophie had moved on so quickly, that he'd really meant that little to her.

Hearing a man answer her phone just once should have been enough to convince him, but apparently he was a slow learner.

"Sorry, wrong—"

"Look, buddy, who are you looking for?" The dude sounded big, his voice rough and deep. Not at all the smooth, suave voice of the kind of man he'd expect Sophie to be with.

Spencer gritted his teeth. What else did he have to lose at this point? "Sophie Olsen?"

"Never heard of her."

Spencer huffed in disbelief. "This is her number."

"No, this is my number." The guy's voice softened. "It's a new number, so maybe . . ."

She had a new number. Which meant she wasn't with this guy. It might not be too late.

But as Spencer clicked off the phone, his elation dissipated.

If she had a new number, he had no way to contact her.

He rubbed his temples. What now?

He'd spent every moment of the week since Tyler had dug the ring out of the junk drawer praying about what to do. He'd been so sure this was God's answer. Contact her. Tell her he loved her. Ask her to give him another chance.

But now he couldn't even find her.

He picked up his phone and did a search for development firms in Chicago. But there were so many. What had she said the name of it was? Something with a heart in it, he was pretty sure.

He scrolled through the listings until he came to Heartland. Could be right.

Without letting himself think, he dialed the number.

"Heartland," a smoothly professional voice answered. What had he expected? That she'd answer her own phone?

"Yes." He tried to sound official. "Sophie Olsen, please."

A pause on the other end. He could hear papers shuffling and wished he could push himself through the telephone to see what was going on there. To see Sophie in her office.

"I'm sorry. There is no Sophie Olsen at this firm."

Spencer's thoughts spun. Another strike out. "I'm sorry I must have the wrong— I thought—" Why was he explaining himself to a complete stranger?

"A Sophie Olsen used to work here." The secretary's voice was almost conspiratorial. "She quit a few days ago."

Spencer pulled at his hair. He was so close. "Could you tell me how to contact her?"

"I'm sorry, I have no forwarding number. But I didn't get the impression she had another job lined up. I think she said something about moving."

Spencer's heart stopped. "Okay, thank you." He hung up without waiting for a reply. That was the end, then. If she was moving, there was no way he'd ever find her.

Unless—

He picked up his phone and scrolled to Violet's number.

"Hey, Spencer." Violet sounded wary. She'd spent the past two months trying to convince him that Sophie had been ready to stay in Hope Springs if he'd asked. But he hadn't believed her—or hadn't wanted to, not if it meant he'd been the one to ruin their chance of being together.

Last time Violet had brought Sophie up, Spencer had bitten her head off and said not to mention her again.

"Look, Violet, I'm sorry about last week. You were right. I do still want to be with her."

He expected a gasp or a cheer or at least some sort of reaction, but Violet was silent.

"Violet? Do you forgive me?" Had he ruined yet another relationship?

"Nothing to forgive. I knew you'd eventually come to your senses. You should call her."

"That's the thing. I tried, but some guy has her number now, and her firm said she quit and is moving."

There was a sharp inhale on the other end of the phone.

"So you didn't know?" Spencer dropped to the couch and cradled his head in his hands.

But he held on to one last shred of hope. "You said she wanted me to ask her to stay. Do you think there's any chance she's coming back here?" He couldn't take a breath as he waited for Violet to say yes, she thought that was exactly what Sophie was doing.

The silence stretched too long. Finally, Violet sighed. "I hope so, Spencer."

"But you don't think so." The words cut at Spencer's throat.

"No, I don't." Violet's voice was gentle. "I'm sorry."

Spencer almost hung up. But he forced himself to ask one more question.

"Do you have her last address?"

# Chapter 32

Sophie sat up straighter in the driver's seat. It was as if she were seeing Hope Springs for the first time. The stores dotting the hillside, the boats dipping up and down in the marina, the lake, bathed in the pinks and oranges of sunset. This was her home. How had she ever doubted it?

A peaceful sensation washed over her. *Thank you for leading me back,* she breathed in silent prayer.

Even the sight of her parents' house didn't leave her with the same tension she'd felt two months ago when she'd come home. She pulled the car to a stop behind the garage and blew out a breath. She hadn't had the nerve to call ahead to let them know she was coming. And now she had to tell them that not only did she want to stay with them indefinitely, but she'd quit at the one thing she'd ever done to make them proud.

Her mother answered the door on the second ring. Her eyes widened at the sight of her daughter on her doorstep, but she took a step back to let Sophie in. "Sophie. This is a surprise." The way she said it, Sophie almost thought she might mean it was a pleasant surprise.

"Sorry to just show up like this." Sophie set her purse on the table in the entryway. She'd left the rest of her stuff in the car for now.

"You're always welcome here. You know that." Sophie stared at her mother. *Did* she know that?

"We were about to eat dinner. Come join us. There's plenty."

We? "Oh, if you have company, I can—"

"What are you talking about? It's just us. Come on, your father will be happy to see you. He thought it was kids selling cookies at the door."

Sophie gaped after her mother's retreating form. Her parents were both home? And eating dinner together? Was she in the right house?

Sophie followed Mom to the kitchen, where she was already pulling out another plate and glass.

"Hey, pumpkin." Sophie's father stood to give her a hug.

It took a moment for her to return it, she was so flabbergasted. "Hi, Dad."

Her mother dished a pile of spaghetti onto her plate and passed it to her. "So to what do we owe this surprise visit?"

Sophie took a big bite, chewing to give herself time to think. But in the end, there was no choice but to tell the truth. "Actually, it's a little more than a visit. I've decided to move back to Hope Springs." They both looked up from their plates in surprise. It was a new sensation, having both of her parents' eyes on her. "I'll find an apartment," she added quickly. "But I was hoping I could stay here until I do."

"What about your job?" Her mother had always been a straight-to-the-point kind of woman.

Sophie swallowed a drink of water. "I quit." She hated how meek her voice was. "I'm sorry. I know you guys are disappointed, but I couldn't—"

"What makes you think we're disappointed?" Her father shoved a bite in his mouth and pointed his fork at her.

"Well, I mean, first— And now I—" She fumbled. Tried again. "But I wasn't happy, and—"

Mom laid down her fork. "If you think being here in Hope Springs will make you happy, then that's what you should do."

Sophie lifted her head, searched Mom's eyes for the judgment she knew would come. But as far as she could tell, Mom was being sincere. Sophie dropped her head and focused on the table, running her fingers over the polished wood.

"Okay, thanks." She couldn't think of anything else to say. She'd been prepared to argue, to defend her choices, to walk away and find somewhere else to stay if she had to. But acceptance—that she wasn't prepared for.

"Do you have any thoughts about what you might do here?" Dad asked.

Sophie shook her head.

"We might have something, if you're interested." With one sentence, Mom offered her what she'd wanted her whole life. What she'd been striving for—their approval.

But she realized now, it wasn't what she needed. "Thanks, but I'm not sure yet what I want to do." Maybe she should tell them about Spencer, too, while they were in an accepting mood, but first she had to see how he felt—if he'd welcome her back as warmly as they had.

Mom got up and rummaged in the fridge, emerging a few seconds later with a cheesecake.

Sophie's mouth watered. "Is that from the Hidden Cafe?"

Her mother nodded. "We actually got it to celebrate."

Sophie looked from one to the other. What was the date? July twentieth. It wasn't either of their birthdays or their anniversary. Not that they usually celebrated that anyway.

"What's the occasion?"

Her parents looked at each other, and Sophie saw something pass between them that she hadn't seen in a long time. Her father laid his hand on top of her mother's, and Sophie fought to keep her mouth from dropping open. "It's been one month since we recommitted to our marriage."

"Recommitted to—?" What did that even mean?

"After you left last time, I read Nana's journal. And I kept thinking about what you said. About shutting the world out." Mom's eyes shone with tears, and Sophie could only stare as Dad tightened his grip on Mom's hand.

Sophie wanted to crawl under the table. She never should have talked to Mom that way. "I'm sorry, I had no right—"

Mom shook her head. "I'm glad you did. It opened my eyes to some things. We've been in counseling together, and it's"—she blew out a breath—"it's going well. We have a long way to go, but we're healing together. In a way we never did before. A way I never let us."

Sophie couldn't wrap her head around what was happening. It seemed impossible this was the same family she'd left two months ago.

"Actually, we wanted to call you, to see if maybe you'd want to talk. If maybe you could forgive us." Mom swiped at a fresh cascade of tears.

Dad cleared his throat. "We realize that a lot of things in our family fell apart after Jordan died." It was the first time Sophie had heard him use her brother's name since the day they'd buried him, and she swallowed against the sudden lump.

"I'm afraid you were the one who suffered a lot of the hurt and anger and confusion I was feeling. Maybe—" The uncertainty in Mom's voice unraveled Sophie, and she had to swipe at her own tears.

"Maybe you'd like to come to counseling with us sometime," Mom finished.

It took a moment before Sophie could answer. "Yeah. I'd like that."

⌒⌒

A mixture of nerves and hope swirled in Sophie's belly.

This was what she'd come back to Hope Springs for. She felt wrung out from last night's emotional reunion with her parents, but in a way, it felt as if that was what she'd needed to be able to face this moment. She drove into Spencer's driveway, trying not to think of the last time she had pulled out of it. Trying not to remember how she'd left him. Again.

It was a lot to ask him to forgive her. To expect him to give her another chance.

But she wasn't going to be too proud to ask for it this time.

She frowned as she stopped in front of Spencer's house. His truck wasn't in the driveway. But her parents had assured her that they hadn't bought the property, after all. Which meant he'd have to be back sometime.

So she'd wait for him.

For as long as it took.

This time, she wasn't going anywhere.

Sophie parked and climbed out of the car, inhaling the soothing scents of cut grass and bee balm. She could stand here and just breathe this air all day.

The sound of little-boy giggles from the backyard drew her attention, and her lips lifted into a smile. She followed the sound and found Tyler chasing his sons across the lawn, tickling them whenever he caught them, then pretending to be defeated and let them go.

Jonah spotted her first and came running over, followed two steps behind by Jeremiah.

Sophie crouched to accept their hugs. Their sticky fingers were warm and welcoming on her bare arms.

"Where'd you go?" Jonah asked. "We missed you."

Sophie ruffled his downy hair. "Sorry about that, buddy. I missed you, too. I had to do some stuff in Chicago, but I'm back now."

"Chicago?" Jeremiah tipped his head at her. "What's that?"

"What are you doing here?" Tyler towered over her, frowning, and Sophie pushed to her feet.

"I'm—" Sophie faltered. She'd been sure Tyler would be on her side. "I came back," she finished lamely.

"I see that. But—"

"Wait, Tyler. Before you go telling me not to break your brother's heart again, let me just say I won't. *I won't.*" Her voice was firm. She was sure this time. "This is where I want to be. He's the one I want to be with. I'm not running anymore."

"Actually—" A slow grin tripped across Tyler's face. "I was just going to say that Spencer isn't here. He's in Chicago. Looking for you."

# Chapter 33

After driving around the block three times, Spencer finally found a parking spot in front of the address Violet had given him.

Sophie's address. If she hadn't moved yet.

He whispered a quick prayer for guidance, then jumped out of his truck and leaned back, lifting a hand to shield his eyes from the glint of the sun off the skyscraper's glass. The building was exactly the kind of place Sophie would choose—all sleek lines and elegance.

He stopped himself from leaping back into his truck and hightailing it out of there. She might think this was the kind of place she belonged, but he knew better. He'd seen her in his workshop, running her hands over their bench. Watched her opening up to friends at the Hidden Cafe. Laughed with her, mud-covered and adorable, in his orchard. The Sophie he knew belonged with him. Whether she knew it yet or not.

Spencer squared his shoulders and marched to the glass doors at the front of the building.

Inside, he pulled up short in the marble-floored lobby. A large fountain in the middle of the room bubbled cheerfully. He squared his shoulders. He may not be able to offer her marble fountains, but he had a bubbling creek just for her.

"Can I help you, sir?"

Spencer turned toward the voice from the other side of the lobby and approached the reception desk. "I'm looking for Sophie Olsen. Could you direct me to her apartment?"

The burly man behind the desk frowned at him. "Do you know Ms. Olsen?"

"Of course I know her. I'm her— We're—" Spencer stopped. What were he and Sophie? They weren't exactly in a relationship right now. But they weren't nothing to each other, either. Spencer debated saying soul mates, but that would sound a little weird.

"I highly doubt that." The man behind the counter spoke as if he'd read Spencer's mind. "If you're so close to her, you'd know she doesn't live here anymore."

Spencer's shoulders fell and all the hope that had sustained him during the five-hour drive to Chicago slithered out of him. He'd known it was a long shot, but he'd been so sure that this was the Lord's plan for him.

"You wouldn't happen to have her new address?"

The look the man gave him said he wouldn't tell Spencer if he did.

He shuffled toward the fountain and sat down, hard, letting his fingers trail in the icy water. *Now what, Lord?*

The prospect of driving home exhausted him.

His phone pealed, but Spencer ignored it, letting it go to voice mail.

Two minutes later, it rang again.

The man behind the reception desk cleared his throat and shot him a pointed look.

Spencer pulled out his phone. Tyler.

His big brother probably wanted an update. Too bad he'd been wrong to think Sophie was sitting down here just waiting for him.

He answered the phone as he pushed out the building's front door.

The sun glared at him, and he ducked his head. "She's not here, Tyler. I was too late." His bitterness shocked even him.

"Spencer."

He froze. It wasn't Tyler.

"Sophie?" He hardly dared think it, and yet he knew her voice better than he knew his own.

"Hi." She sounded breathless and light and full of laughter. Spencer tipped his face toward the heavens, letting the warmth of the sun wash over him.

"Wait." His head snapped back to earth. "How are you on Tyler's phone? Where are you?"

"I'm in Hope Springs. I'm at your house."

Spencer's head spun. "But why?" She was moving to who knows where. So why was she in Hope Springs? At his house?

Sophie laughed again, and the sound filled him. "I was under the impression you'd be here."

"You were looking for me?" Spencer closed his eyes. Was this really happening?

"I was looking for you, Spencer." Her voice was soft, a gentle caress.

He leaned against the building. The elegant building she'd just moved out of. To go somewhere better, no doubt. "And then where are you going?"

Silence on the other end. So he'd hit the nail on the head then.

"I'm not going anywhere," she said after what felt like forever. "I'm staying right here."

Spencer pushed off the cool wall and strode toward his truck. "Then what am I still doing here?"

# Chapter 34

Sophie watched the giant machine wrap its metal arms around the cherry tree. A canvas tarp stretched from the machine to circle the tree trunk like giant bat wings. With a vigorous shake, the cherries toppled from the tree into the tarp. A moment later, the machine's arms had retracted, folding up the tarp and neatly sending the cherries onto a conveyor belt that led to a series of cold-water tanks at the back of the truck. She plucked four cherries off the belt, then handed one each to Jonah and Jeremiah and popped another in her mouth.

"I saw that." Spencer smiled as he climbed down from the cherry picker and walked over.

She held out the last cherry. "It's okay. I held on to one as a bribe."

He took it but didn't eat it. Instead, he leaned down to give her a deep kiss. She wrapped her arms around his neck and pulled him closer. If she lived a hundred years, she'd never get tired of kissing this man.

"All right, enough of that." Tyler's mock-stern voice carried to them. "There are children here."

Sophie laughed as Spencer pulled away.

"Actually—" Tyler gave Spencer a look Sophie couldn't read. "These munchkins need some lunch anyway. How about we take a break?"

"Goodie!" Jonah cried. "Can we have Aunt Sophie mac 'n' cheese again?"

"Hey!" Tyler put on an offended face. "I can cook."

They'd been harvesting together all week, and Sophie had made the boys mac 'n' cheese two days in a row already. Apparently, the gloppy mess she made of it appealed to them more than their dad's burnt noodles.

"Sure." Sophie reached to grab their hands.

Spencer cleared his throat. "Actually, I was hoping we could have a picnic today."

"Yay!" Both boys danced around Spencer, chanting, "Picnic, picnic!"

"Boys!" Tyler had to yell to be heard over them. They both stopped and turned big eyes on him. "I think Uncle Spencer wants to have a picnic with just Aunt Sophie."

The boys directed their pitiful gazes at Spencer. Sophie gave his arm a light shove. There was no way he'd be able to resist them.

But he ruffled their hair and told them to have a good lunch.

"You can come next time," Sophie called after them as they followed their father toward the house, stopping to pick up the cherries that had fallen in the grass along the way.

"That was nice of your brother. To give us some time alone." They hadn't had much of that since Spencer had come rushing home from Chicago and swept her up in his arms. The harvest had kept them all busy. But Sophie had enjoyed every moment of it.

"Yeah, he's a prince," Spencer said wryly. He ducked his head into the cab of the cherry picker and emerged a few seconds later holding a picnic basket. "Actually, he's been a lifesaver. I don't think I could have bought this place without him." His eyes were on her, and she knew he was waiting. She'd already apologized for telling her parents to make an offer on the place. But she needed to say more.

"I'm glad you bought it, Spencer. It's your heritage. And I know how much you love it. Plus—" She plucked another cherry out of the water. "I really think you'll make it successful."

Spencer lashed the picnic basket to the ATV. "Thank you." He held a hand out to her, and she took it. "That means a lot."

They both climbed onto the vehicle.

"So where are we going?"

"You'll see." Spencer turned the ignition and revved the engine, and they were off.

She pressed herself into him, wrapping her arms around his waist and letting her head fall on his back. Never in her wildest dreams had she thought she'd be giving up a prestigious job to ride around a farm clinging to the back of an ATV. But she'd never felt more at home.

The creek was low this time, barely splashing them, and after ten minutes or so, Spencer throttled the vehicle down. The trees were in full leaf now, and she couldn't see through to the clearing. But she knew where they were.

They were going to have lunch under the hidden blossom tree. A flutter of nerves tickled her stomach. The location felt significant after all Spencer had told her about his family's history here.

She waited for Spencer to unfasten the picnic basket, then they walked hand-in-hand through the trees.

When they emerged into the clearing, she caught her breath. Red burst from every inch of the hidden blossom tree, and the branches swept low to the ground, heavy with cherries. The ripened fruit was almost more breathtaking than the delicate blossoms had been in spring.

Spencer parted two branches and gestured for her to duck into the tree's shade. Inside, light dappled the ground and fell on—

"The bench!" Sophie gasped and lunged for it, running her fingers over its smooth surface. "How did you—"

But Spencer took her hands and spun her so her back was to the bench, then gently lowered her to sit.

The moment felt familiar all at once, and her hand flew to cover her mouth. Was this really happening?

"Sophie—" Spencer's whisper caressed her. She could feel the love in it—see the love reflected in his eyes.

He reached into the picnic basket and pulled out a small, black box.

Sophie's eyes filled before he'd even dropped to one knee in front of her. Spencer opened the box.

The ring inside sparkled at her, but Sophie only glanced at it for a moment.

She couldn't take her eyes off Spencer's face.

"Sophie Olsen." Spencer's voice was strong now, sure. "You are everything I have ever wanted. Everything I have ever imagined. Everything I could ever need. Will you let me be the same for you? Will you marry me?"

Sophie remembered the last time he had asked. How her insides had quivered with fear. How she'd felt the need to run. To hide. How she'd known she could never live up to the perfect wife he deserved.

She still knew she couldn't. But this time she knew he'd love her anyway. Just like she'd love him.

"I will."

Spencer laughed out loud and pulled her to the ground next to him, crushing her against his chest.

He leaned back slightly and slipped the ring onto her finger.

"I will never stop loving you." His voice told her it was true.

She watched the light dance off the ring. "Not until forever?"

Spencer lowered his head toward hers.

His words were a breath against her lips. "Not even then."

Thank you for reading NOT UNTIL FOREVER! I hope you loved Sophie and Spencer's story! Catch up with them as their friends Jared and Peyton find love in Not Until This Moment, another sweet, second-chance story set in Hope Springs!

And be sure to sign up for my newsletter to get Ethan and Ariana's story, NOT UNTIL CHRISTMAS, as a free gift.

Visit https://www.valeriembodden.com/gift or use the QR code below to join.

## *A preview of* NOT UNTIL THIS MOMENT (Hope Springs book 2)

### Chapter 1

Peyton wiped her frosting-smudged hands on her apron and eased the kitchen door open to peek into the empty ballroom. Her eyes roamed the elegant table settings, the tall vases filled with amaryllis and orchids, the fairy lights that floated above the room like stars. The bride and groom were at the church, probably exchanging their vows at this very moment, but soon they'd come into this perfect room. Peyton could picture exactly how the bride's face would look. She'd seen that look on every bride's face at every wedding she'd ever been to. It was the look that said this was the happiest day of her life.

Peyton pulled her head back and let the door close, barely suppressing a sigh.

A year ago, she'd thought her own happily ever after was just around the corner. But now it seemed further away than ever.

Leah bustled past with a stack of serving bowls. She shuffled them and reached over to pat Peyton's arm, the same way she had at every wedding they'd worked together in the past year.

Peyton straightened her shoulders and marched to the counter. Standing here dwelling on regrets wouldn't get the cake done.

She surveyed the four tiers she'd already stacked and grabbed her bench scraper to smooth the spots where her fingers had left impressions in the buttercream, exposing the red velvet swirl underneath. It was exactly what she would have picked for her own wedding cake—if Jared had ever proposed.

She blinked against the sting behind her eyelids. She had to stop feeling this way every time she set up a wedding cake. It'd been almost a year since he'd told her he never intended to get married. Almost a year since she'd decided she couldn't be with a man who couldn't commit to a future with her. Almost a year since she'd pulverized her own heart when she'd broken up with him.

*Time to move on.*

With a sudden decisiveness, she grabbed her piping materials and filled them with the buttercream she was becoming famous for. Okay, maybe not famous, but well-known enough around Hope Springs to keep her busy most weekends of the summer and even a few in winter—like this one. She set to work adding the delicate beading the couple had requested for the edges of their cake. She let the noises around her fade as she concentrated on making each tiny circle perfect, just barely connecting it to the next one. The intense focus was soothing.

"You're coming to Tamarack with us next weekend, right?" Leah's voice right next to her made Peyton jump, and she almost yanked the piping tip back from the cake. Fortunately, years of practice had given her a steady hand, even in the face of Leah's enthusiasm. She finished the last four beads, then pulled the tip away and spun the cake to examine her work. Not too bad.

"It's perfect." Leah pretended to swipe a finger toward the frosting, but Peyton batted her hand away.

"Tell me you're coming, or I'll do it." Leah held a finger toward the cake again, her eyebrows waggling as if daring Peyton to tempt her.

Too bad Peyton knew it was an empty threat. Leah didn't have an unkind bone in her body, and she'd never ruin Peyton's work—or a couple's wedding cake.

"I don't think so." Peyton couldn't meet Leah's eyes. She hated to disappoint anyone, least of all the friend who'd come to feel like a sister, but there was no way she could go on the annual skiing trip. Not if Jared was going to be there. And anyway, he was the only reason she'd been invited in the first place. Now that they weren't together, it would be awkward if she tagged along.

"Sawyer specifically told me to make sure you knew you were still invited." Drat Leah's ability to read her mind.

"I'm sure he was only being polite."

Unlike the others who went on the trip every year, Peyton hadn't grown up in Hope Springs. She'd only met Sawyer a few years ago when she'd gone with Jared and his friends to the ski resort Sawyer's family owned.

"Well, if he was, then saying no would be rude." Leah gave her an impish smile, obviously certain she'd won the argument.

But Peyton was tougher than that. "I have another wedding that weekend." Which also happened to be Valentine's Day. Not that she cared about her former favorite holiday anymore.

"I know. I'm catering that one, too. But we'll be back by Wednesday. Try again."

Peyton reviewed her mental calendar. Why couldn't she come up with something else?

"So it's really about Jared." Leah gave her the same half-sympathetic, half-stern look she did every time Jared's name came up.

Peyton snatched her scraper and smoothed a nonexistent dent. Of course it was about Jared. "Don't you have a wedding dinner to get ready?"

Leah planted a hand on her hip. "You said you were over Jared."

She had said that. Multiple times. She'd told it to herself every day, hoping that one of these days it would be true.

"I am over him. I just—"

"Then prove it." Leah crossed her arms in front of her. "If you're over him, you won't have a problem coming skiing with all of us. Maybe you'll meet someone new."

Peyton studied her friend. She should say no. Leah was intentionally pushing her buttons. But her friend knew her well. Knew she was incapable of backing down from a challenge.

"Fine," she huffed. "I'll come. Now let me finish this cake."

Leah gave her a triumphant smile and a quick squeeze. "Gotta run. I have a wedding dinner to prepare." She rushed to the other side of the kitchen, where the rest of her crew worked to unload carts filled with chicken, potatoes, and all kinds of food that made Peyton's mouth water.

Peyton shook her head and tried to force her concentration back to her work. This was one challenge she should have walked away from.

## Chapter 2

Jared drove the monstrous conversion van he'd just picked up into the parking lot of the Hidden Cafe.

He'd been waiting for this Friday morning for weeks now. He was ready for this ski trip like he'd been ready for few things in his life. The past year had been rough, and he needed to get out of Hope Springs for a few days. Just enough time to clear his head. To escape the constant fear of running into Peyton. To finally get over her.

*As if that will ever happen.*

But it had to happen. Peyton had made it clear what she wanted—marriage, a life together, a family. Much as he would do anything to give her the moon and stars, the thing she was asking for—that was the one thing he couldn't give her.

Which didn't stop him from glancing around the parking lot, just in case her car was here.

That sinking feeling in his stomach when he didn't spot it was stupid. He'd known she wouldn't come this year. Or any year, now that they weren't together.

He turned off the vehicle and jumped out. Anyway, it was for the best, he reminded himself as he strode into the Hidden Cafe.

The moment he stepped through the door, he stopped to inhale deeply, just as he did whenever he came here. The scents of home cooking got him every time. His home had never smelled like this growing up.

It had smelled more like . . .

Did fear have a smell?

"Hey, man." Ethan clapped a hand on his shoulder. "Got some muffins for the road." He opened the paper bag in his hand and pulled out a giant muffin, passing it to Jared.

"Thanks." Jared took a big bite of the still-warm pastry, savoring the apple and cinnamon melting on his tongue. "Everyone here?"

"Just about. Ariana's over there." Ethan glowed at the mere mention of his wife's name. "And Leah. Her brother Dan is coming, too. I guess he just moved back to town to serve with his dad at the church."

Jared nodded shortly. He didn't need to know what was going on at the church.

"Emma's on her way. And Sophie and Spencer just called. They'll be here in a few minutes, and they're bringing Spencer's brother Tyler. Vi can't make it this year. She didn't want to close the store."

Jared tallied the group in his head. "So we've got five here, and we're waiting for four."

"Actually—" Ethan cleared his throat and didn't meet Jared's eyes. "We're waiting for five."

Jared did a quick recount. "I only count four."

"That's because you're not counting Peyton."

"Pey—" Jared ran a hand up and down his rough cheek. "Peyton's coming?" His throat went dry. He'd been so sure she wouldn't come. So sure he'd be able to use this time to get over her.

Ethan watched him. "You okay with that?"

Jared gave a tight smile and a quick nod. "Of course."

But Ethan tipped his head to the side. His partner on the volunteer first responder squad knew him better than anyone else. Knew how hard not being with Peyton had been for him. He was the only one who knew why Jared would never marry, too.

"Well, I guess I'm going to have to be, aren't I?" he muttered as the door opened and Peyton stepped inside.

Jared caught his breath as her eyes landed on his for a second, then skipped away. Her mouth was set into a faint scowl as she gazed past him, clearly searching for someone else—probably anyone else.

He shuffled to the side to get out of her way. No reason to make this harder than it had to be.

Her lips curled into a smile, and for half a heartbeat he let himself think it was for him. But she slid past him and let Leah wrap her into a hug.

Jared tried not to think about how long it had been since his arms had been around Peyton. Tried not to notice how they ached to hold her again.

*So far so good on being okay with this.*

He moved toward the door. "We should get the van loaded." He said it loudly so everyone would hear, but his gaze locked on Peyton and refused to budge. She wore the white ski jacket with pink trim he had helped her pick out the first year they'd gone skiing together. Her pale hair was swept into some kind of messy bun on top of her head, making her look casual and sophisticated at the same time. And her eyes. Her eyes were what had drawn him to her in the first place. So impossibly light they were almost transparent. But it was more than their color. It was their warmth. Their sincerity. The way they revealed everything she felt.

Which was also what scared him about them.

He held the door as Ethan and Ariana filed past, then waited for the others.

But Leah was introducing Peyton to a dark-haired guy with his back to Jared.

When Peyton smiled at the guy and held out a hand to shake his, Jared's stomach clenched. He'd been waiting for the moment he learned she'd met someone else. But that didn't mean he wanted to witness it.

His eyes flicked to hers again. But all he saw in them was polite interest as she talked to the stranger.

After a second, the three of them moved toward the door. Caught watching them, Jared considered making an escape out to the van. But he couldn't very well close the door in their faces.

He stood his ground as they approached.

Peyton passed through first, barely acknowledging him, though he was pretty sure he heard a mumbled "thanks" before she scooted toward the van. That woman couldn't bear to be impolite, even to him.

"Hey, Jared." He tore his eyes off Peyton's retreating figure and forced them to Leah. "You remember my little brother Dan? He was a couple years behind us in school."

Little brother? The guy easily stood two inches taller than Jared's six feet.

The guy gave Jared a warm smile and held out a hand. "Thanks for letting me tag along."

Jared returned the handshake. "No problem." *As long as you don't steal my girlfriend.*

But that wasn't right. If Dan ended up with Peyton, he wouldn't be stealing her. Jared had already let her go.

Too bad his heart didn't know that yet.

Outside, Sophie, Spencer, Tyler, and Emma were getting out of their cars. Jared opened the back of the van and everyone stashed their bags, exchanging greetings and laughs as they did. Only Peyton seemed quiet.

The moment he opened the doors of the van, she launched herself inside and scooted to the corner of the backseat.

Clearly, she wasn't going to be riding shotgun this year.

Jared waited for the others to load into the vehicle, then jumped in, glancing at Leah, who'd taken the seat next to him.

"We ready for this?" Jared turned the ignition as a resounding chorus of yeses hit his ears.

As he backed out of the spot, his eyes flicked to the rearview mirror. They landed instantly on Peyton, but she was staring out the window, her lips drawn into a thin line.

He was tempted to tell a stupid joke, the way he had a hundred times before to erase that look from her face. But this time he was pretty sure hearing from him would only make the line thinner.

## KEEP READING NOT UNTIL THIS MOMENT

# More Books by Valerie M. Bodden

## Hope Springs

*While the books in the Hope Springs series are linked, each is a complete romance featuring a different couple.*

Not Until Forever (Sophie & Spencer)

Not Until This Moment (Jared & Peyton)

Not Until You (Nate & Violet)

Not Until Us (Dan & Jade)

Not Until Christmas Morning (Leah & Austin)

Not Until This Day (Tyler & Isabel)

Not Until Someday (Grace & Levi)

Not Until Now (Cam & Kayla)

Not Until Then (Bethany & James)

Not Until The End (Emma & Owen)

## River Falls

*While the books in the River Falls series are linked, each is a complete romance featuring a different couple.*

Pieces of Forever (Joseph & Ava)

Songs of Home (Lydia & Liam)

Memories of the Heart (Simeon & Abigail)

Whispers of Truth (Benjamin & Summer)

Promises of Mercy (Judah & Faith)

## River Falls Christmas Romances

*Wondering about some of the side characters in River Falls who aren't members of the Calvano family? Join them as they get their own happily-ever-afters in the River Falls Christmas Romances.*

Christmas of Joy (Madison & Luke)

## Want to know when my next book releases?

You can follow me on Amazon to be the first to know when my next book releases! Just visit amazon.com/author/valeriembodden and click the follow button.

# Acknowledgements

As in all things, my first thanks must go to my heavenly father, who has so richly blessed me in every way—and most of all in his assurance that my worth is found not in myself but in Christ. What a rich promise! And what an amazing blessing to be able to write books that share his word with you, my wonderful readers. I am fully aware of what a privilege he has given me in this writing life, and I thank him for it every day.

And a super huge thank you to my husband, who proposed to me on a park bench and who later made me a bench engraved with our initials. It makes me smile every time I see it. I'm so grateful for the life God has given us together—and for the four children he has blessed us with. This mama is so thankful to have kiddos who cheer her on and support her.

A heartfelt thank you also goes out to my amazing Advance Reader Team: Josie Bartelt, Jennifer Ellenson, Rachel Kozinski, Connie Gronholz, Jamie Lee, Janice Petersen, and Korin Thomas. These ladies provided priceless feedback and encouragement as I prepared to send this book out into the world, and I am forever grateful to them.

And, of course, thank you to *you*, dear reader. I'm grateful that you have chosen to spend your time with these characters who have become so dear to my heart. I look forward to sharing more stories with you.

May God bless and keep you.

# About the Author

Valerie M. Bodden has three great loves: Jesus, her family, and books. And chocolate (okay, four great loves). She is living out her happily ever after with her high-school-sweetheart-turned-husband and their four children. Her life wouldn't make a terribly exciting book, as it has a happy beginning and middle, and someday when she goes to her heavenly home, it will have a happy end.

She was born and raised in Wisconsin but recently moved with her family to Texas, where they're all getting used to the warm weather (she doesn't miss the snow even a little bit, though the rest of the family does) and saying y'all instead of you guys.

Valerie writes emotion-filled Christian fiction that weaves real-life problems, real-life people, and real-life faith. Her characters may (okay, will) experience some heartache along the way, but she will always give them a happy ending.

Feel free to stop by www.valeriembodden.com to say hi. She loves visitors! And while you're there, you can sign up for your free story.

Made in United States
North Haven, CT
30 June 2024

54251701R00162